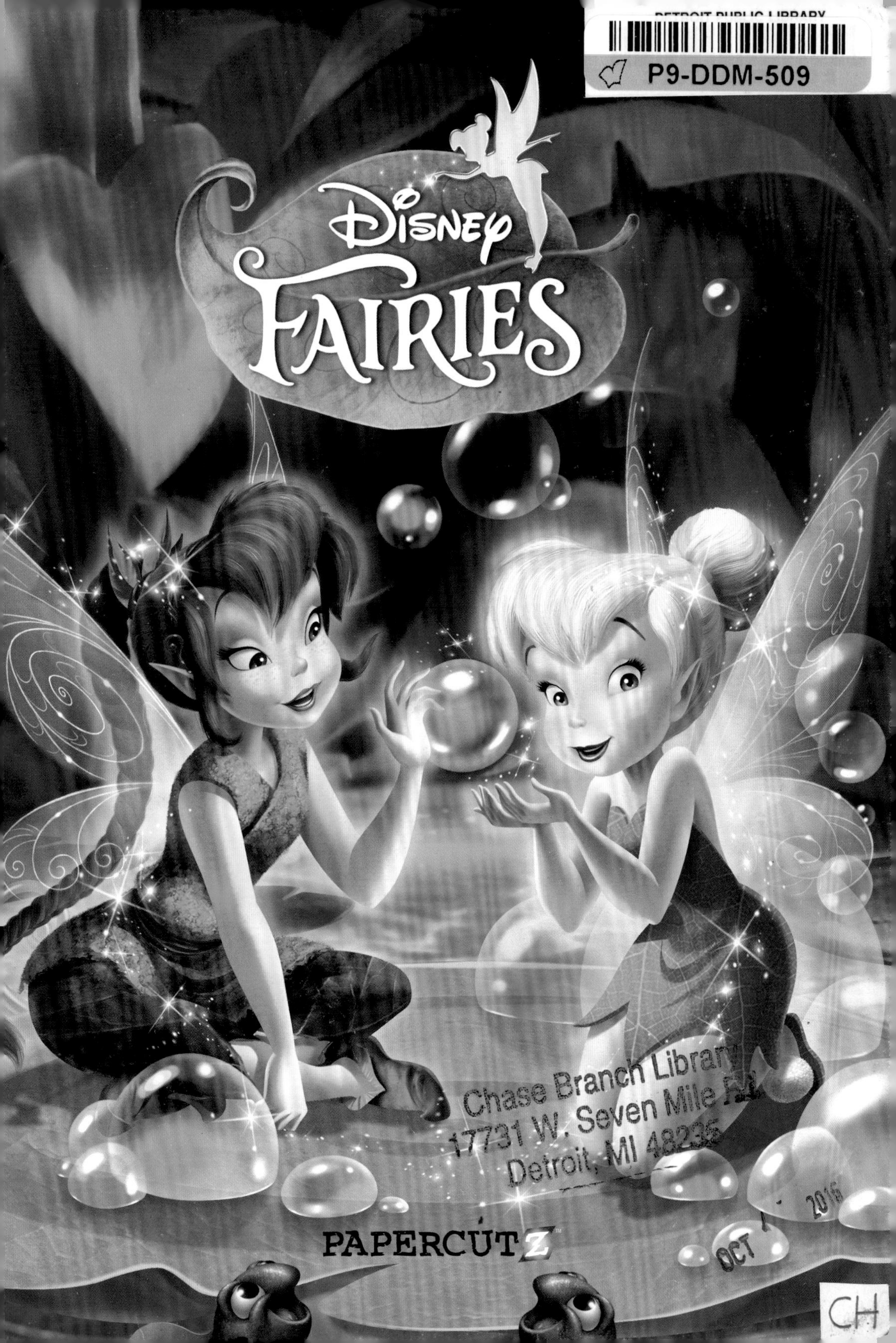
Disney
FAIRIES
PAPERCUTZ

Graphic Novels Available from

PAPERCUTZ

Graphic Novel #1
"Prilla's Talent"

Graphic Novel #2
"Tinker Bell and the
Wings of Rani"

Graphic Novel #3
"Tinker Bell and the Day
of the Dragon"

Graphic Novel #4
"Tinker Bell
to the Rescue"

Graphic Novel #5
"Tinker Bell and
the Pirate Adventure"

Graphic Novel #6
"A Present
for Tinker Bell"

Graphic Novel #7
"Tinker Bell the
Perfect Fairy"

Graphic Novel #8
"Tinker Bell and her
Stories for a Rainy Day"

Graphic Novel #9
"Tinker Bell and
her Magical Arrival"

Graphic Novel #10
"Tinker Bell and
the Lucky Rainbow"

Graphic Novel #11
"Tinker Bell and the
Most Precious Gift"

Graphic Novel #12
"Tinker Bell and the
Lost Treasure"

Graphic Novel #13
"Tinker Bell and the
Pixie Hollow Games"

Graphic Novel #14
"Tinker Bell and Blaze"

**Tinker Bell and the
Great Fairy Rescue**

Graphic Novel #15
"Tinker Bell and the
Secret of the Wings"

COMING SOON

Graphic Novel #16
"Tinker Bell and the
Pirate Fairy"

Disney FAIRIES

#11 "Tinker Bell and the Most Precious Gift"

Contents

PAPERCUTZ™

NEW YORK

"Where There's a Dream, There's a Way"
Concept and Script: Carlo Panaro
Revised Dialogue: Cortney Faye Powell
Pencils: Manuela Razzi
Inks: Roberta Zanotta
Color: Studio Kawaii
Letters: Janice Chiang
Page 5 art:
Concept: Tea Orsi
Pencils and Inks: Sara Storino
Color: Andrea Cagol

"The Starlight Harvest"
Concept and Script: Tea Orsi
Revised Dialogue: Cortney Faye Powell
Pencils: Manuela Razzi
Inks: Marina Baggio
Color: Studio Kawaii
Letters: Janice Chiang
Page 18 Art:
Concept: Tea Orsi
Pencils and Inks: Sara Storino
Color: Andrea Cagol

"The Most Precious Gift"
Concept and Script: Carlo Panaro
Revised Dialogue: Cortney Faye Powell
Layout: Benedetta Barone
Pencils: Caterina Giogetti
Inks: Roberta Zanotta
Color: Studio Kawaii
Letters: Janice Chiang
Page 31 Art:
Concept: Tea Orsi
Pencils and Inks: Sara Storino
Color: Andrea Cagol

"A Prickly Problem"
Concept and Script: Tea Orsi
Revised Dialogue: Cortney Faye Powell
Art: Sara Storino
Color: Studio Kawaii
Letters: Janice Chiang
Page 44 Art:
Concept: Tea Orsi
Pencils and Inks: Sara Storino
Color: Andrea Cagol

"Rosetta's Night Out"
Concept and Script: Tea Orsi
Revised Dialogue: Jim Salicrup
Layout: Benedetta Barone
Pencils: Caterina Giogetti
Inks: Cristina Giorgilli
Color: Studio Kawaii
Letters: Janice Chiang

Production – Nelson Design Group, LLC
Special Thanks – Shiho Tilley
Production Coordinator – Beth Scorzato
Associate Editor – Michael Petranek
Jim Salicrup
Editor-in-Chief

ISBN: 978-1-59707-394-3 paperback edition
ISBN: 978-1-59707-395-0 hardcover edition

Papercutz books may be purchased for business or promotional use. For information on bulk purchases please contact Macmillan Corporate and Premium Sales Department at (800) 221-7945 x5442.

Printed in China
September 2014 by Asia One Printing LTD
13/F Asia One Tower
8 Fung Yip St., Chaiwan
Hong Kong

Distributed by Macmillan

Third Papercutz Printing

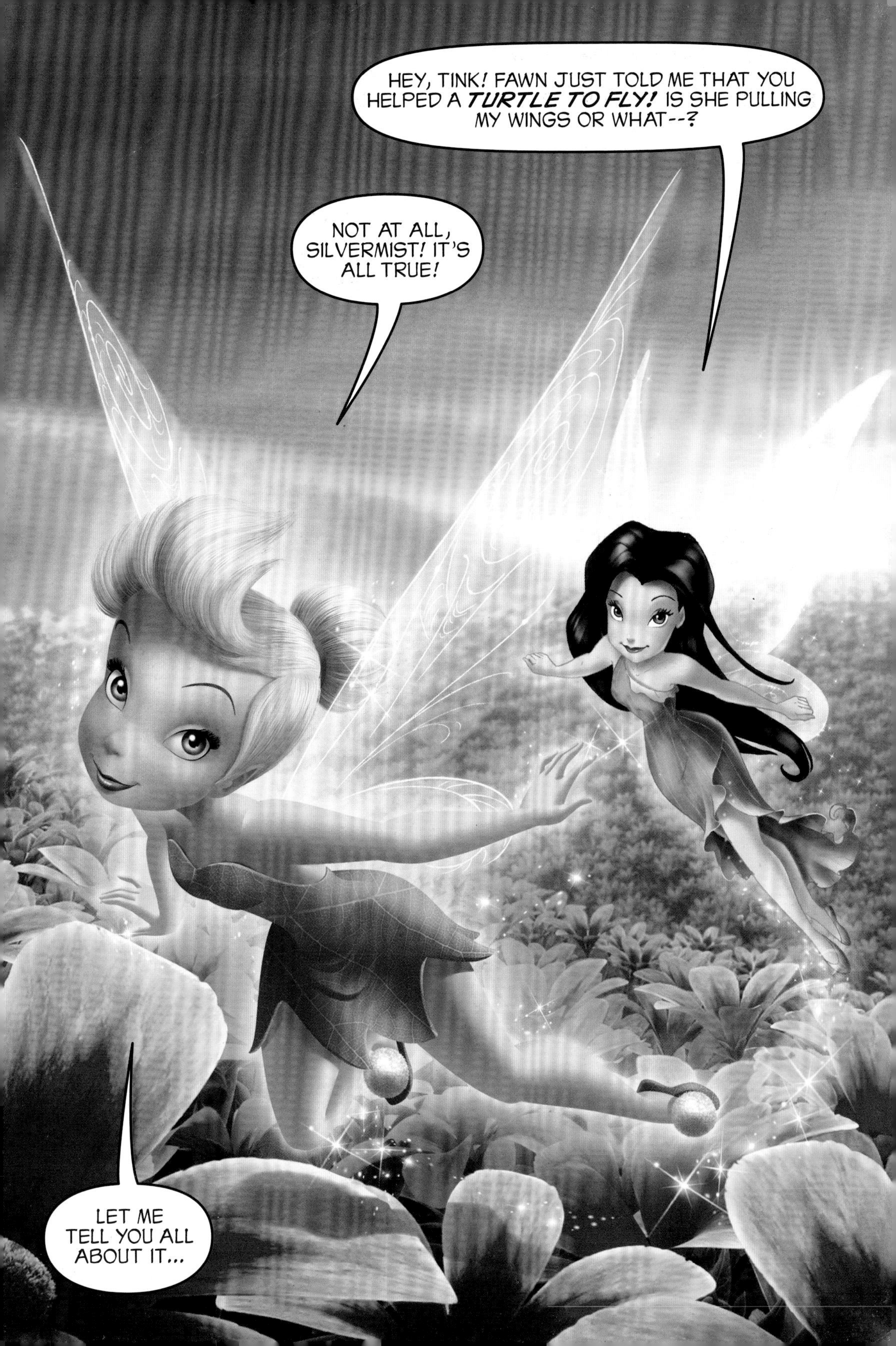
HEY, TINK! FAWN JUST TOLD ME THAT YOU HELPED A TURTLE TO FLY! IS SHE PULLING MY WINGS OR WHAT--?
NOT AT ALL, SILVERMIST! IT'S ALL TRUE!
LET ME TELL YOU ALL ABOUT IT...

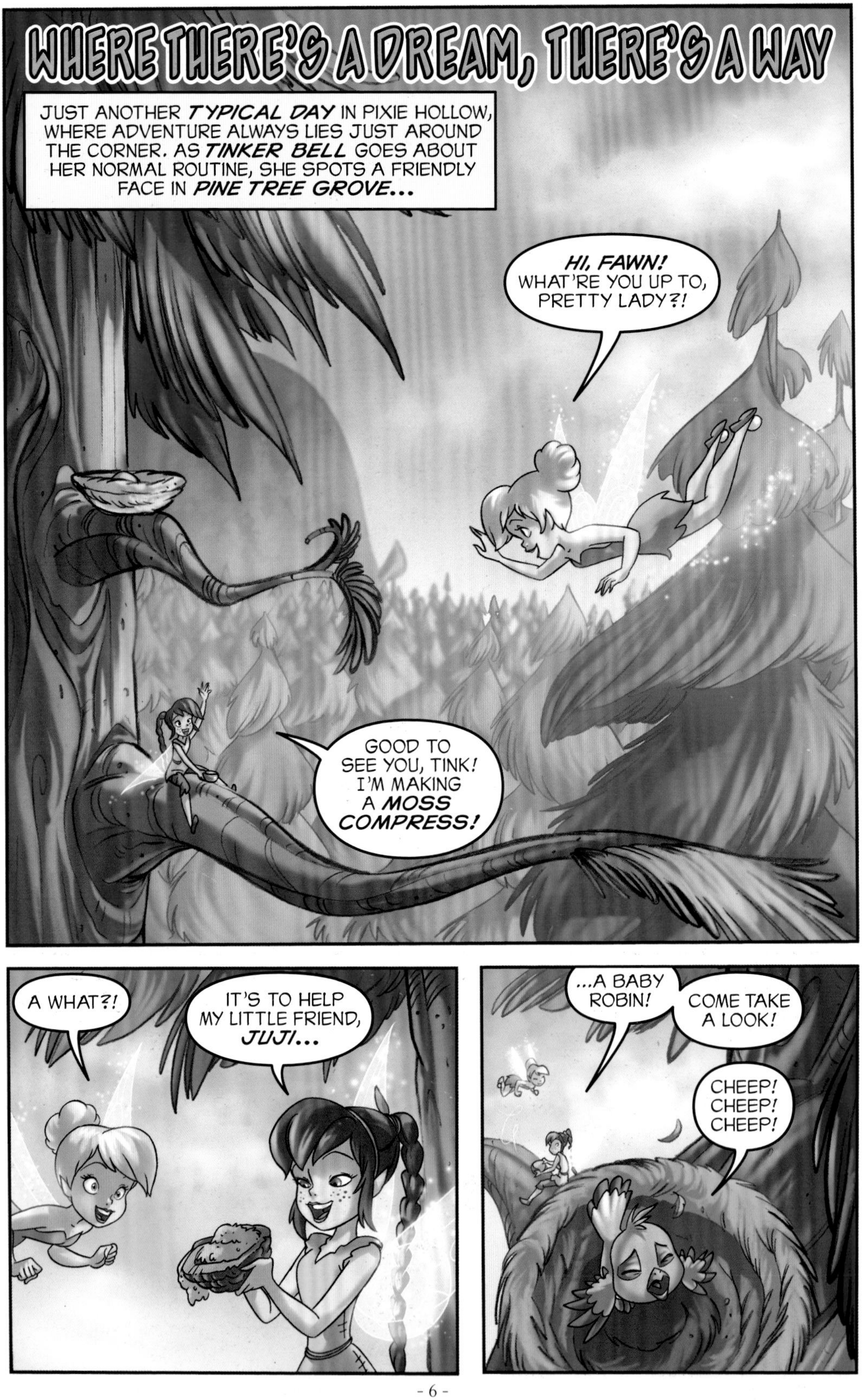
WHERE THERE'S A DREAM, THERE'S A WAY
JUST ANOTHER TYPICAL DAY IN PIXIE HOLLOW, WHERE ADVENTURE ALWAYS LIES JUST AROUND THE CORNER. AS TINKER BELL GOES ABOUT HER NORMAL ROUTINE, SHE SPOTS A FRIENDLY FACE IN PINE TREE GROVE...
HI, FAWN! WHAT'RE YOU UP TO, PRETTY LADY?!
GOOD TO SEE YOU, TINK! I'M MAKING A MOSS COMPRESS!
A WHAT?!
IT'S TO HELP MY LITTLE FRIEND, JUJI...
...A BABY ROBIN!
COME TAKE A LOOK!
CHEEP! CHEEP! CHEEP!

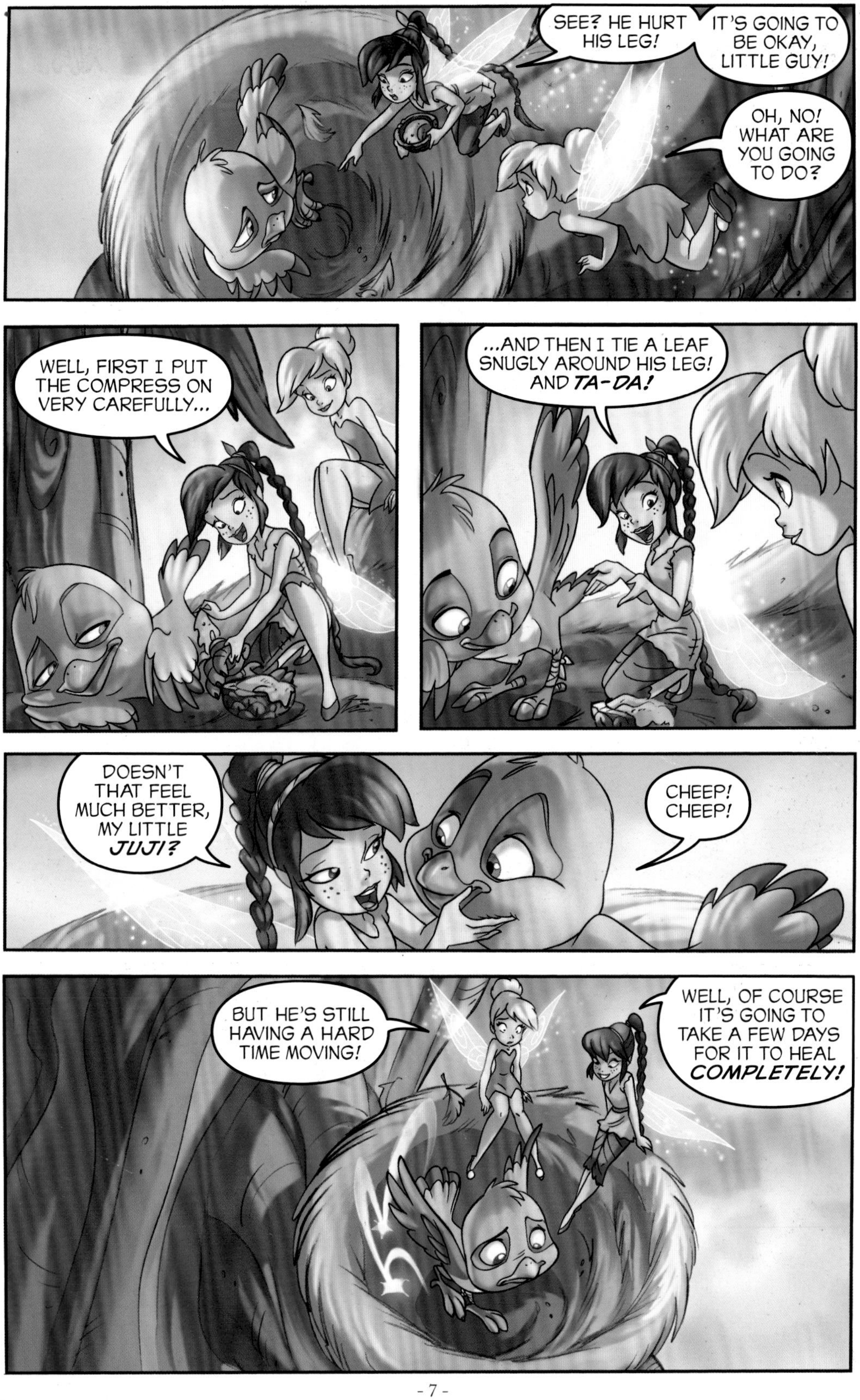
SEE? HE HURT HIS LEG!
IT'S GOING TO BE OKAY, LITTLE GUY!
OH, NO! WHAT ARE YOU GOING TO DO?
WELL, FIRST I PUT THE COMPRESS ON VERY CAREFULLY...
...AND THEN I TIE A LEAF SNUGLY AROUND HIS LEG! AND TA-DA!
DOESN'T THAT FEEL MUCH BETTER, MY LITTLE JUJI?
CHEEP! CHEEP!
BUT HE'S STILL HAVING A HARD TIME MOVING!
WELL, OF COURSE IT'S GOING TO TAKE A FEW DAYS FOR IT TO HEAL COMPLETELY!

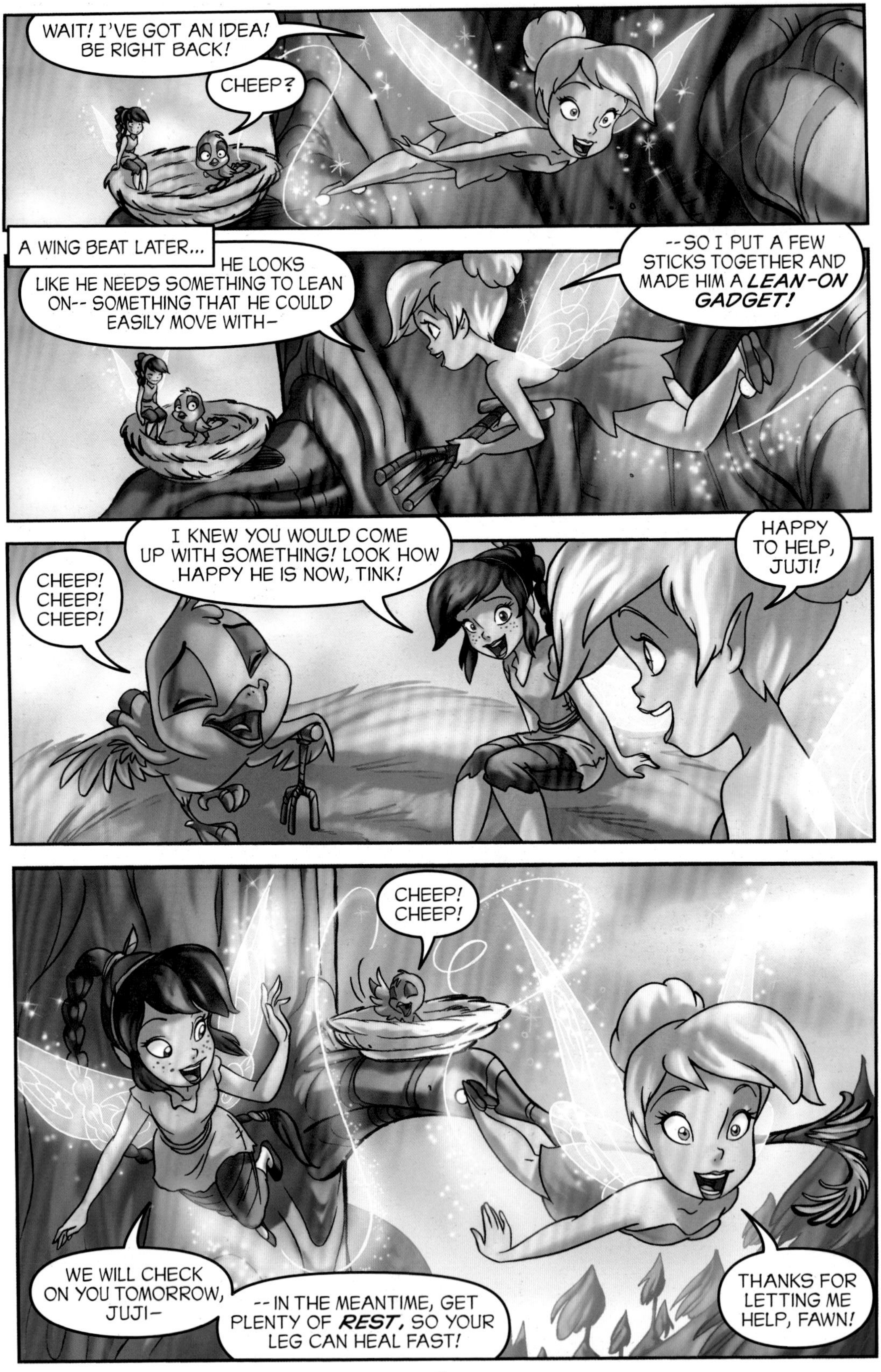
WAIT! I'VE GOT AN IDEA! BE RIGHT BACK!
CHEEP?
A WING BEAT LATER...
HE LOOKS LIKE HE NEEDS SOMETHING TO LEAN ON-- SOMETHING THAT HE COULD EASILY MOVE WITH-
--SO I PUT A FEW STICKS TOGETHER AND MADE HIM A LEAN-ON GADGET!
CHEEP! CHEEP! CHEEP!
I KNEW YOU WOULD COME UP WITH SOMETHING! LOOK HOW HAPPY HE IS NOW, TINK!
HAPPY TO HELP, JUJI!
CHEEP! CHEEP!
WE WILL CHECK ON YOU TOMORROW, JUJI-
--IN THE MEANTIME, GET PLENTY OF REST, SO YOUR LEG CAN HEAL FAST!
THANKS FOR LETTING ME HELP, FAWN!

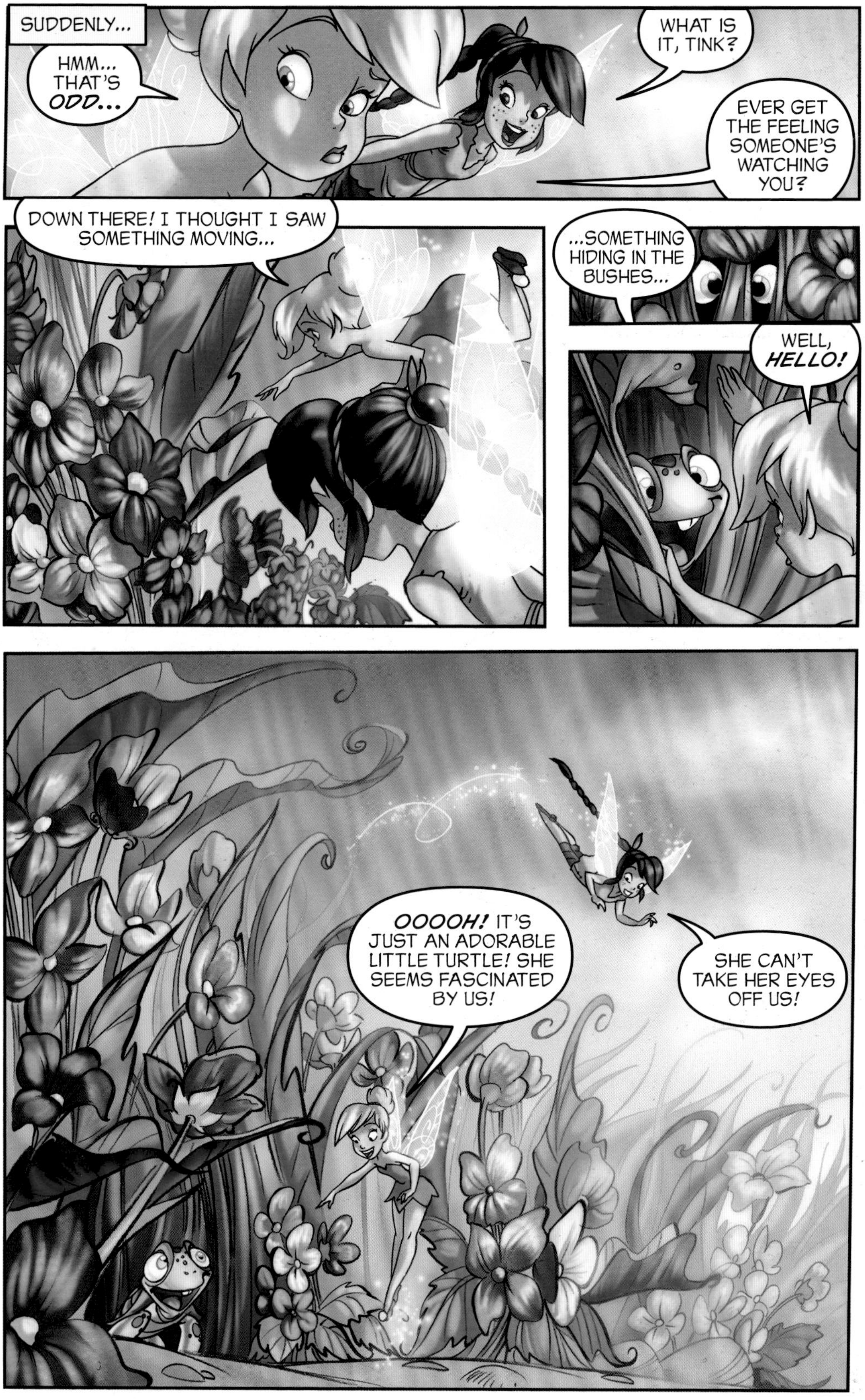
SUDDENLY...
HMM... THAT'S ODD...
WHAT IS IT, TINK?
EVER GET THE FEELING SOMEONE'S WATCHING YOU?
DOWN THERE! I THOUGHT I SAW SOMETHING MOVING...
...SOMETHING HIDING IN THE BUSHES...
WELL, HELLO!
OOOOH! IT'S JUST AN ADORABLE LITTLE TURTLE! SHE SEEMS FASCINATED BY US!
SHE CAN'T TAKE HER EYES OFF US!

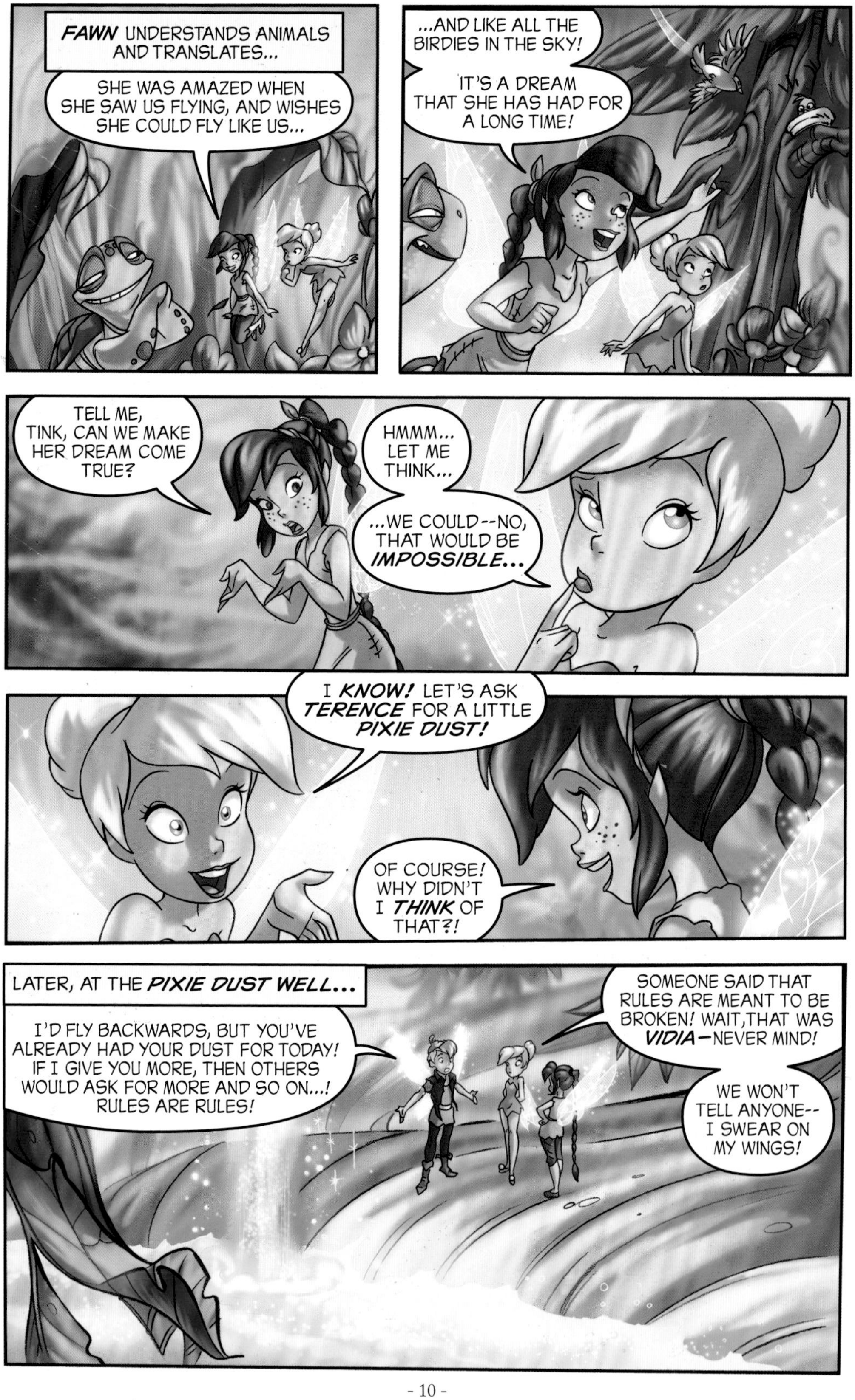
FAWN UNDERSTANDS ANIMALS AND TRANSLATES...
SHE WAS AMAZED WHEN SHE SAW US FLYING, AND WISHES SHE COULD FLY LIKE US...
...AND LIKE ALL THE BIRDIES IN THE SKY!
IT'S A DREAM THAT SHE HAS HAD FOR A LONG TIME!
TELL ME, TINK, CAN WE MAKE HER DREAM COME TRUE?
HMMM... LET ME THINK...
...WE COULD--NO, THAT WOULD BE IMPOSSIBLE...
I KNOW! LET'S ASK TERENCE FOR A LITTLE PIXIE DUST!
OF COURSE! WHY DIDN'T I THINK OF THAT?!
LATER, AT THE PIXIE DUST WELL...
I'D FLY BACKWARDS, BUT YOU'VE ALREADY HAD YOUR DUST FOR TODAY! IF I GIVE YOU MORE, THEN OTHERS WOULD ASK FOR MORE AND SO ON...! RULES ARE RULES!
SOMEONE SAID THAT RULES ARE MEANT TO BE BROKEN! WAIT, THAT WAS VIDIA—NEVER MIND!
WE WON'T TELL ANYONE-- I SWEAR ON MY WINGS!

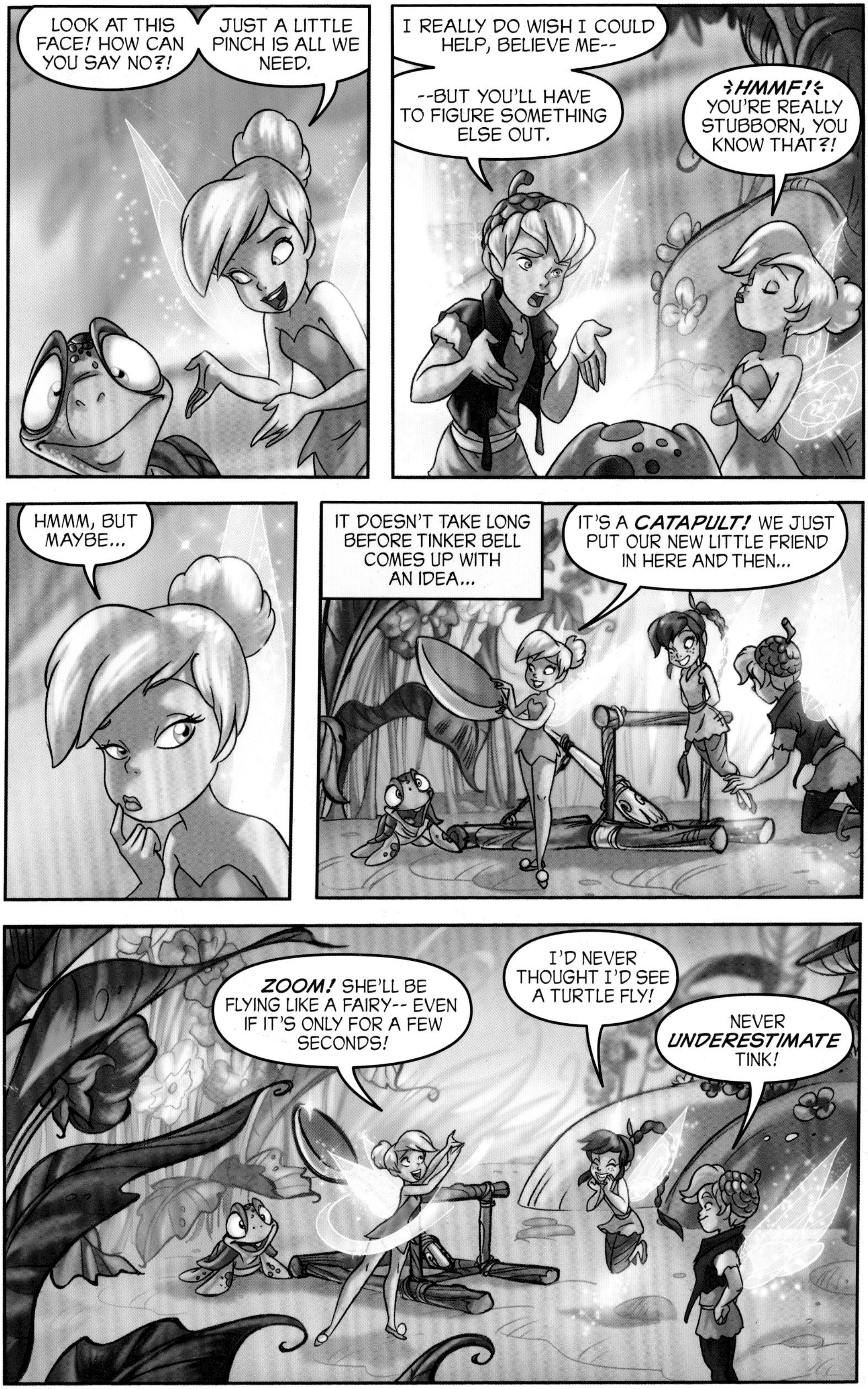

LOOK AT THIS FACE! HOW CAN YOU SAY NO?!
JUST A LITTLE PINCH IS ALL WE NEED.
I REALLY DO WISH I COULD HELP, BELIEVE ME--
--BUT YOU'LL HAVE TO FIGURE SOMETHING ELSE OUT.
HMMF! YOU'RE REALLY STUBBORN, YOU KNOW THAT?!
HMMM, BUT MAYBE...
IT DOESN'T TAKE LONG BEFORE TINKER BELL COMES UP WITH AN IDEA...
IT'S A CATAPULT! WE JUST PUT OUR NEW LITTLE FRIEND IN HERE AND THEN...
ZOOM! SHE'LL BE FLYING LIKE A FAIRY-- EVEN IF IT'S ONLY FOR A FEW SECONDS!
I'D NEVER THOUGHT I'D SEE A TURTLE FLY!
NEVER UNDERESTIMATE TINK!

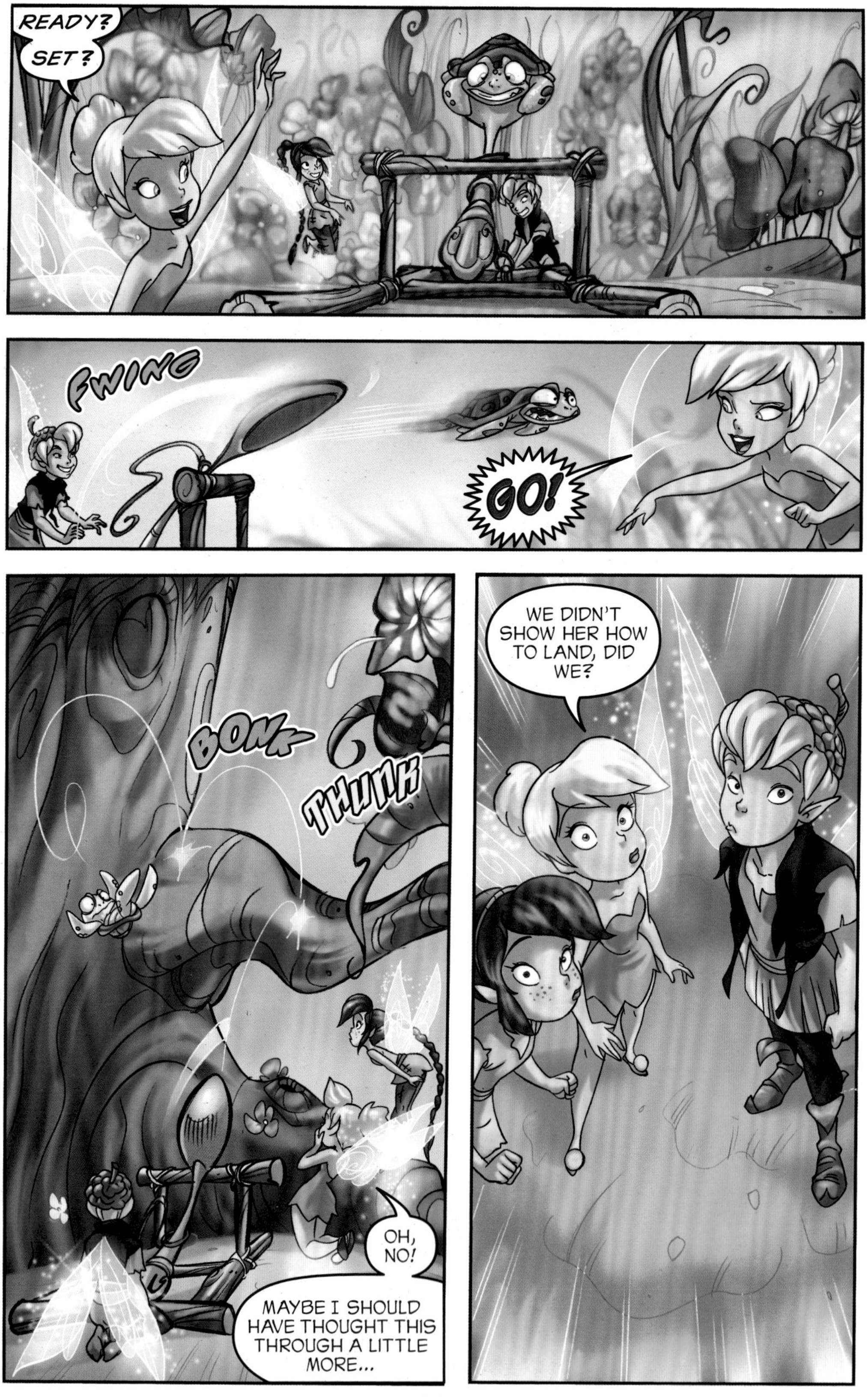
READY?
SET?
FWING
GO!
BONK
THUNK
OH, NO!
MAYBE I SHOULD HAVE THOUGHT THIS THROUGH A LITTLE MORE...
WE DIDN'T SHOW HER HOW TO LAND, DID WE?

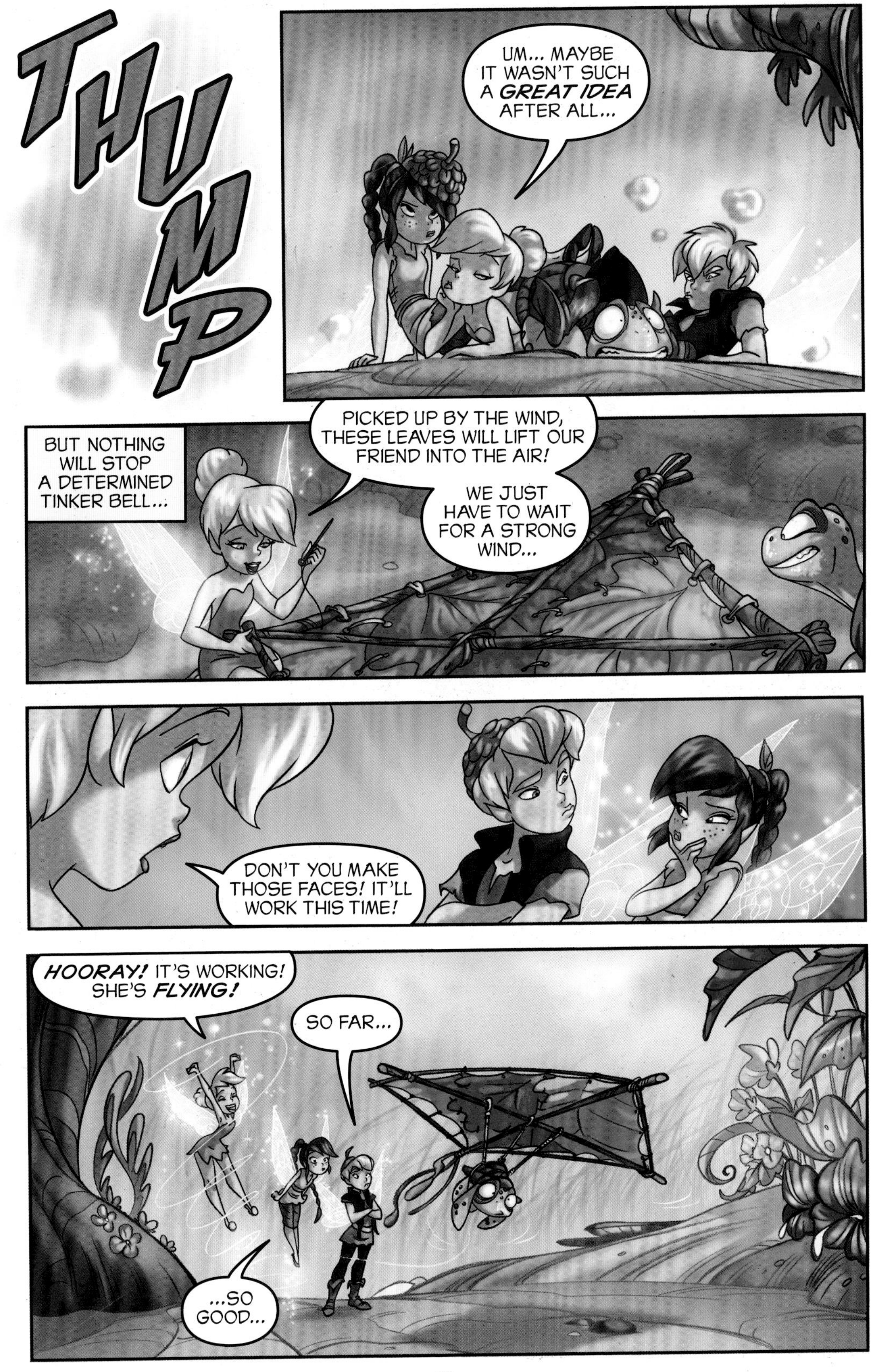
THUMP
UM... MAYBE IT WASN'T SUCH A GREAT IDEA AFTER ALL...
BUT NOTHING WILL STOP A DETERMINED TINKER BELL...
PICKED UP BY THE WIND, THESE LEAVES WILL LIFT OUR FRIEND INTO THE AIR!
WE JUST HAVE TO WAIT FOR A STRONG WIND...
DON'T YOU MAKE THOSE FACES! IT'LL WORK THIS TIME!
HOORAY! IT'S WORKING! SHE'S FLYING!
SO FAR...
...SO GOOD...

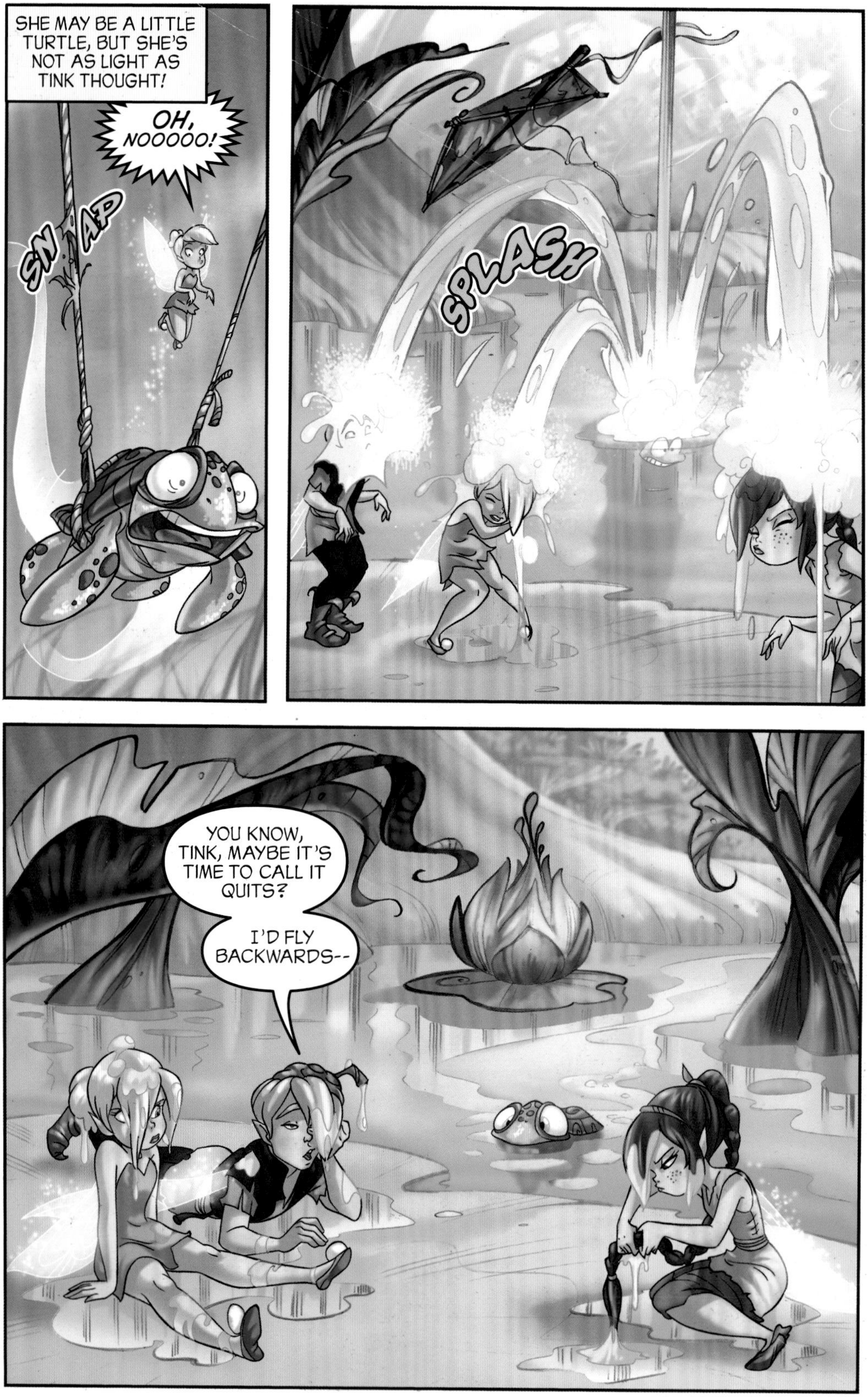
SHE MAY BE A LITTLE TURTLE, BUT SHE'S NOT AS LIGHT AS TINK THOUGHT!
OH, NOOOOO!
SNAP
SPLASH
YOU KNOW, TINK, MAYBE IT'S TIME TO CALL IT QUITS?
I'D FLY BACKWARDS--

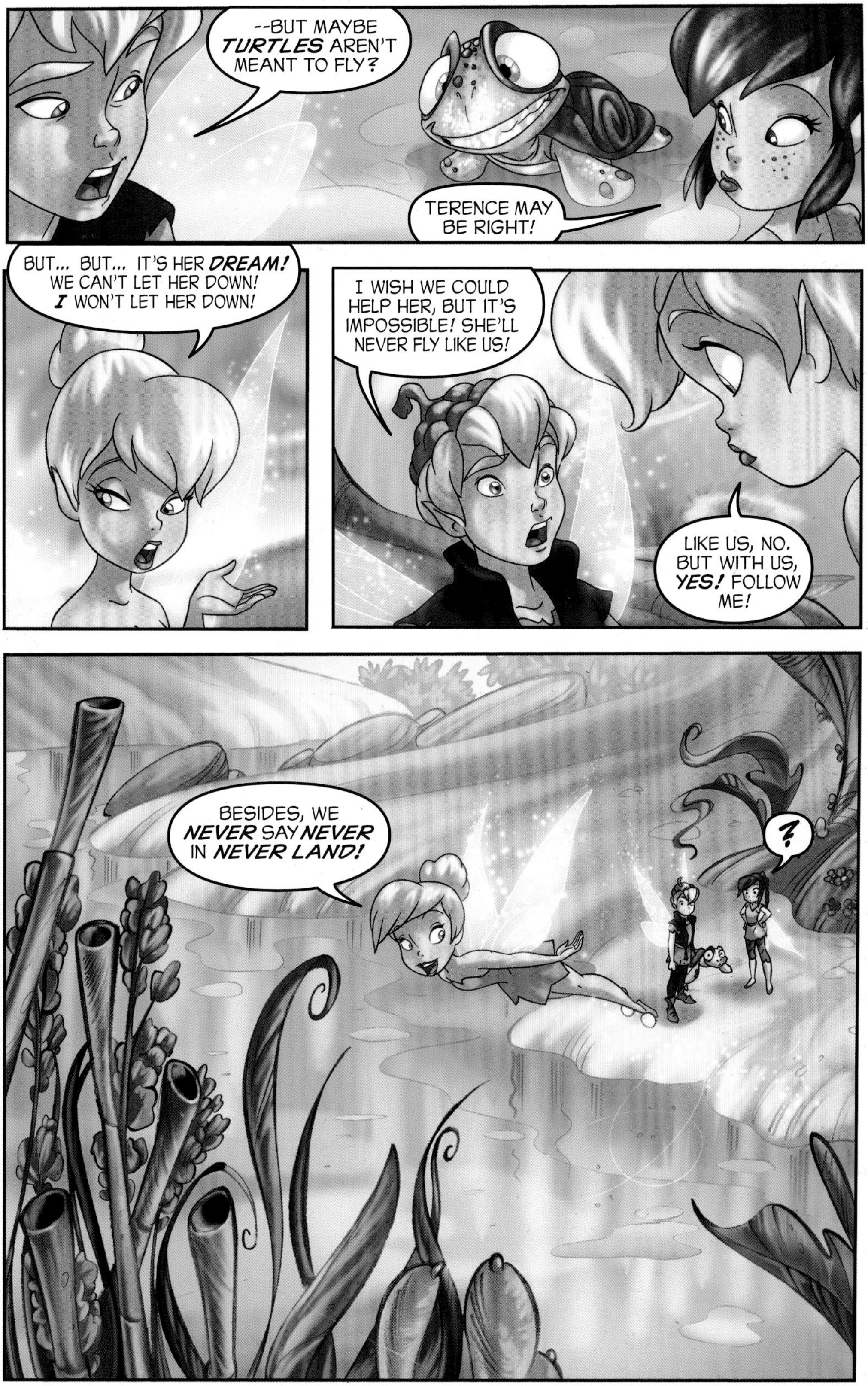
--BUT MAYBE TURTLES AREN'T MEANT TO FLY?
TERENCE MAY BE RIGHT!
BUT... BUT... IT'S HER DREAM! WE CAN'T LET HER DOWN! I WON'T LET HER DOWN!
I WISH WE COULD HELP HER, BUT IT'S IMPOSSIBLE! SHE'LL NEVER FLY LIKE US!
LIKE US, NO. BUT WITH US, YES! FOLLOW ME!
BESIDES, WE NEVER SAY NEVER IN NEVER LAND!
?

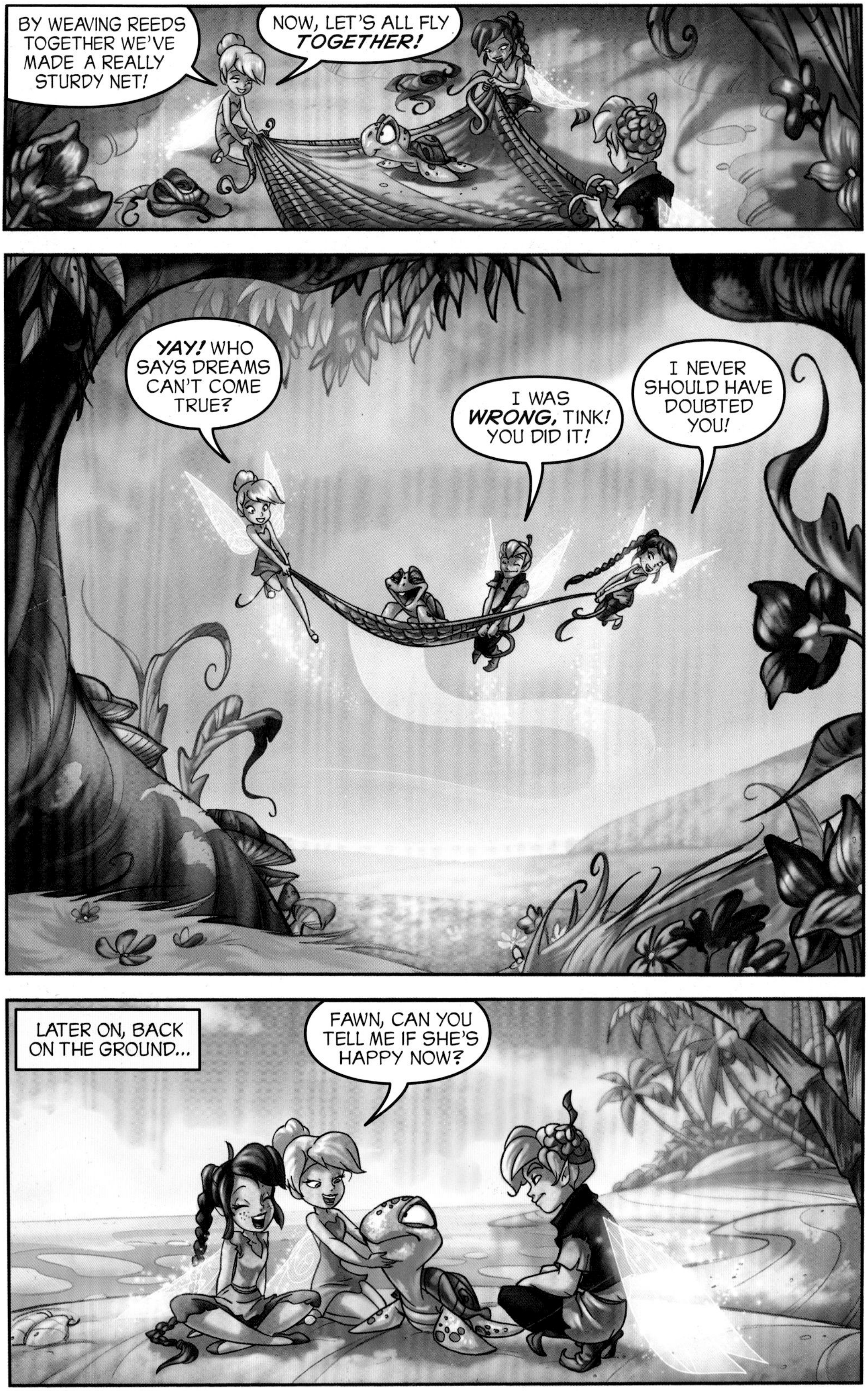
BY WEAVING REEDS TOGETHER WE'VE MADE A REALLY STURDY NET!
NOW, LET'S ALL FLY *TOGETHER!*
YAY! WHO SAYS DREAMS CAN'T COME TRUE?
I WAS *WRONG,* TINK! YOU DID IT!
I NEVER SHOULD HAVE DOUBTED YOU!
LATER ON, BACK ON THE GROUND...
FAWN, CAN YOU TELL ME IF SHE'S HAPPY NOW?

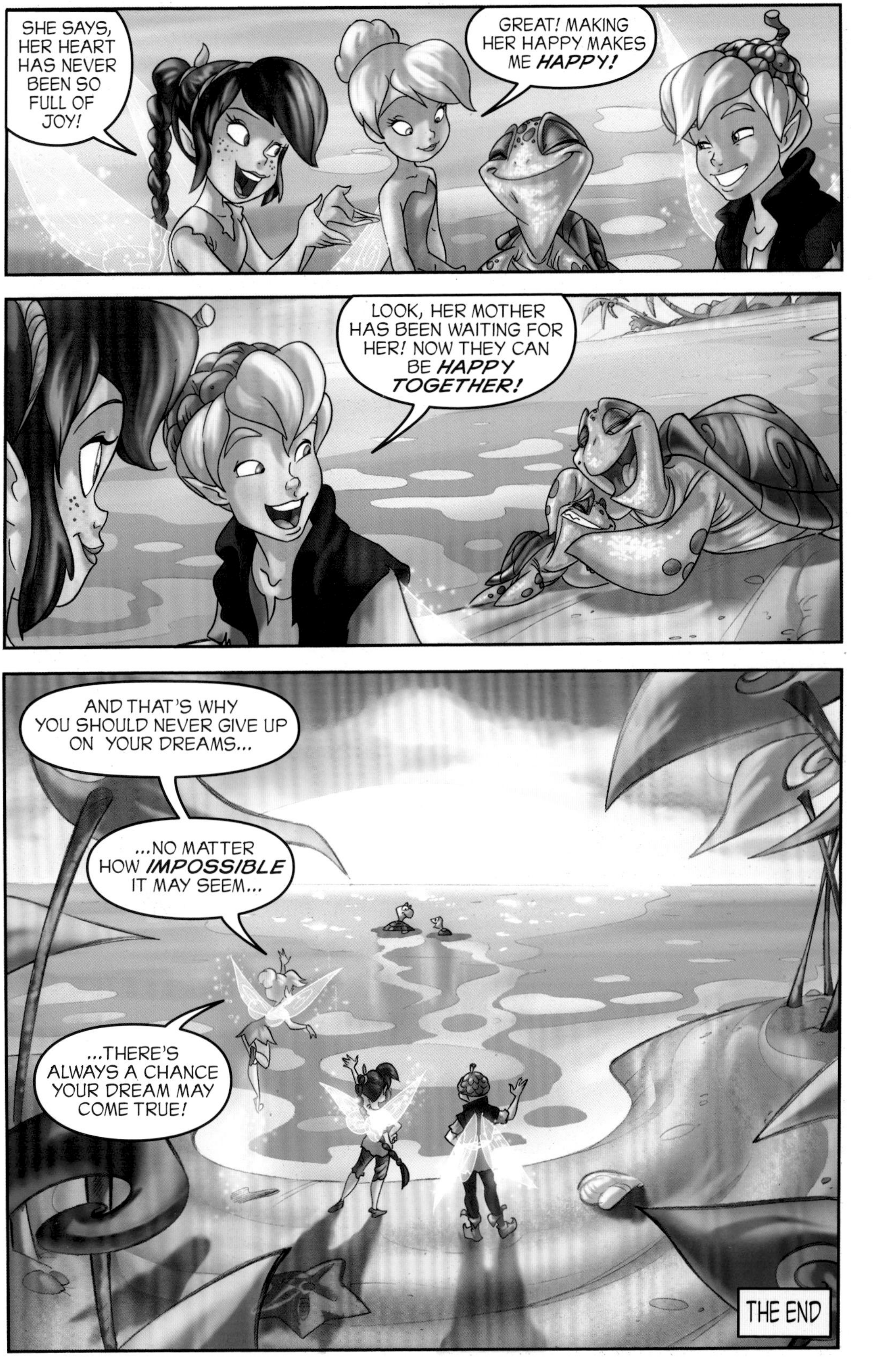
SHE SAYS, HER HEART HAS NEVER BEEN SO FULL OF JOY!
GREAT! MAKING HER HAPPY MAKES ME *HAPPY!*
LOOK, HER MOTHER HAS BEEN WAITING FOR HER! NOW THEY CAN BE *HAPPY TOGETHER!*
AND THAT'S WHY YOU SHOULD NEVER GIVE UP ON YOUR DREAMS...
...NO MATTER HOW *IMPOSSIBLE* IT MAY SEEM...
...THERE'S ALWAYS A CHANCE YOUR DREAM MAY COME TRUE!
THE END

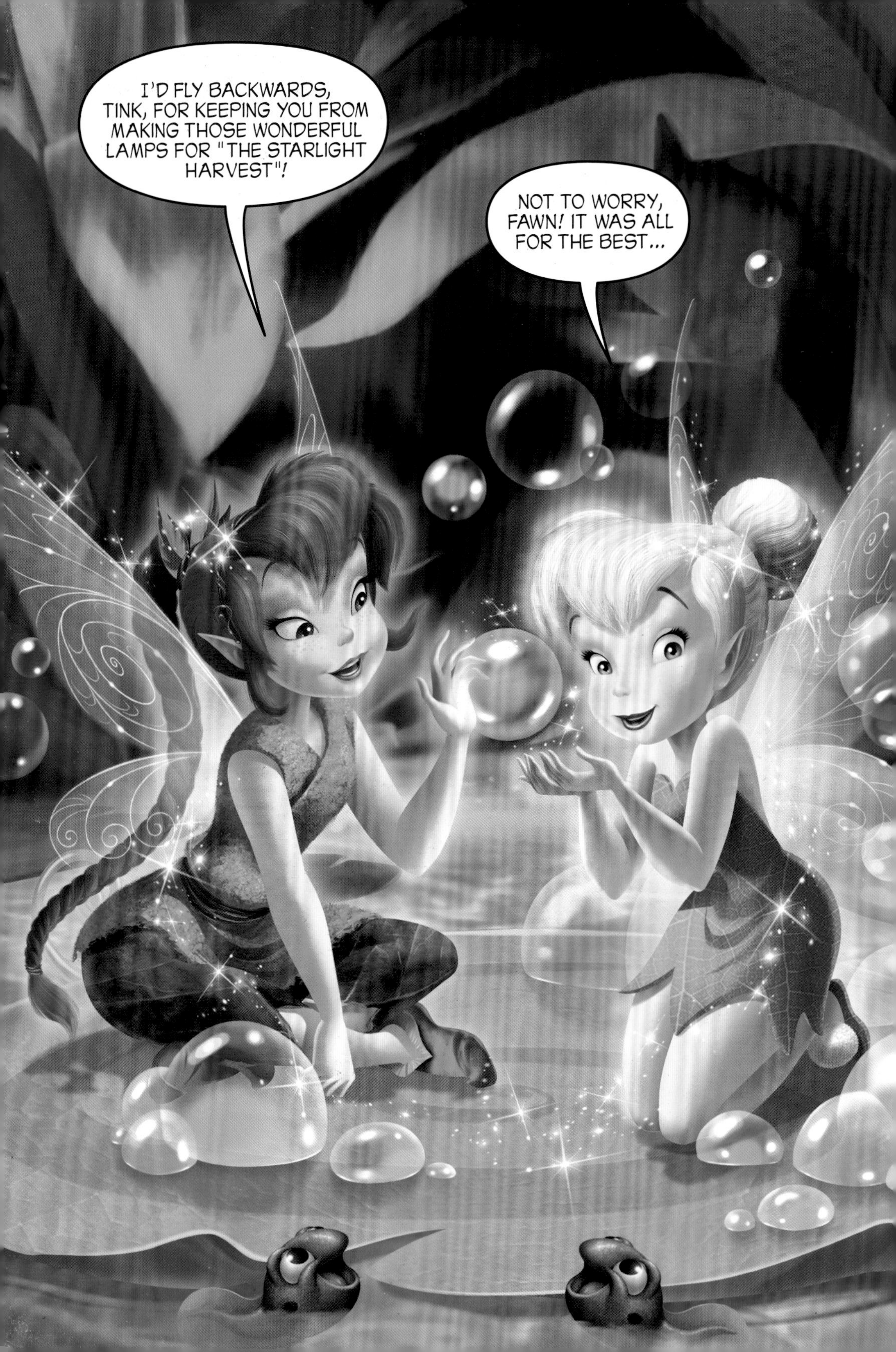
I'D FLY BACKWARDS, TINK, FOR KEEPING YOU FROM MAKING THOSE WONDERFUL LAMPS FOR "THE STARLIGHT HARVEST"!
NOT TO WORRY, FAWN! IT WAS ALL FOR THE BEST...

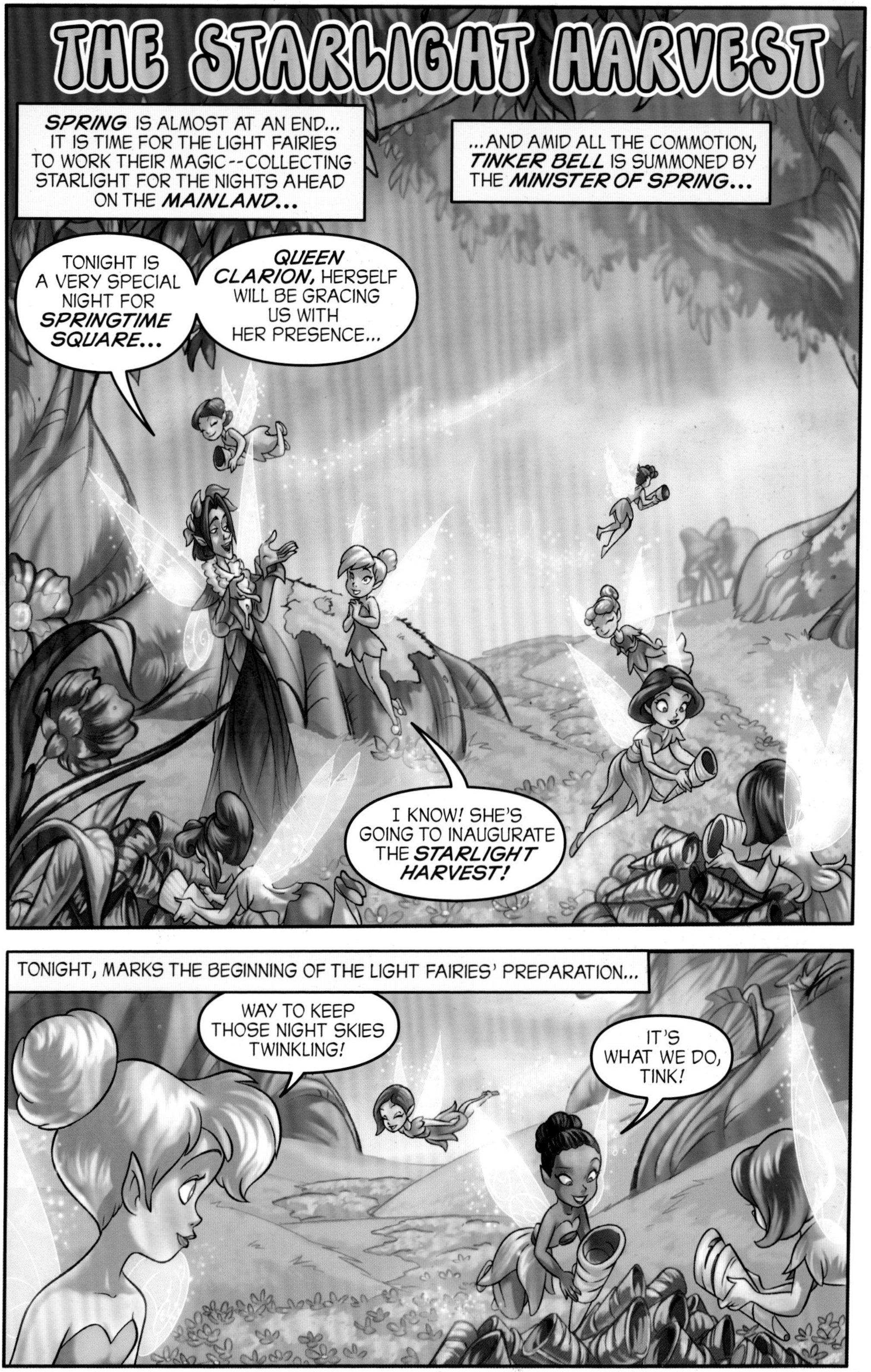
THE STARLIGHT HARVEST
SPRING IS ALMOST AT AN END... IT IS TIME FOR THE LIGHT FAIRIES TO WORK THEIR MAGIC--COLLECTING STARLIGHT FOR THE NIGHTS AHEAD ON THE MAINLAND...
...AND AMID ALL THE COMMOTION, TINKER BELL IS SUMMONED BY THE MINISTER OF SPRING...
TONIGHT IS A VERY SPECIAL NIGHT FOR SPRINGTIME SQUARE...
QUEEN CLARION, HERSELF WILL BE GRACING US WITH HER PRESENCE...
I KNOW! SHE'S GOING TO INAUGURATE THE STARLIGHT HARVEST!
TONIGHT, MARKS THE BEGINNING OF THE LIGHT FAIRIES' PREPARATION...
WAY TO KEEP THOSE NIGHT SKIES TWINKLING!
IT'S WHAT WE DO, TINK!

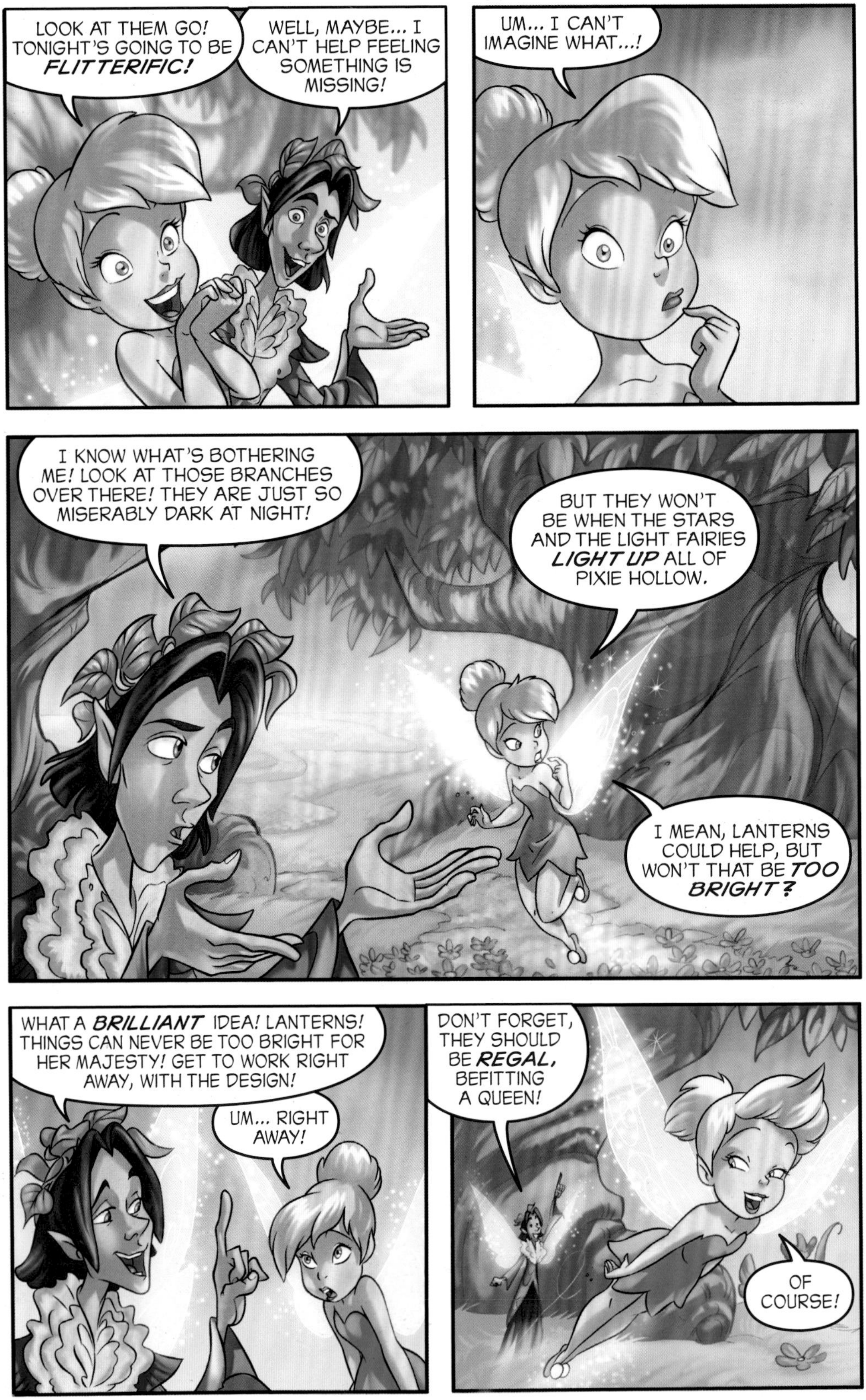

LOOK AT THEM GO! TONIGHT'S GOING TO BE FLITTERIFIC!
WELL, MAYBE... I CAN'T HELP FEELING SOMETHING IS MISSING!
UM... I CAN'T IMAGINE WHAT...!
I KNOW WHAT'S BOTHERING ME! LOOK AT THOSE BRANCHES OVER THERE! THEY ARE JUST SO MISERABLY DARK AT NIGHT!
BUT THEY WON'T BE WHEN THE STARS AND THE LIGHT FAIRIES LIGHT UP ALL OF PIXIE HOLLOW.
I MEAN, LANTERNS COULD HELP, BUT WON'T THAT BE TOO BRIGHT?
WHAT A BRILLIANT IDEA! LANTERNS! THINGS CAN NEVER BE TOO BRIGHT FOR HER MAJESTY! GET TO WORK RIGHT AWAY, WITH THE DESIGN!
UM... RIGHT AWAY!
DON'T FORGET, THEY SHOULD BE REGAL, BEFITTING A QUEEN!
OF COURSE!

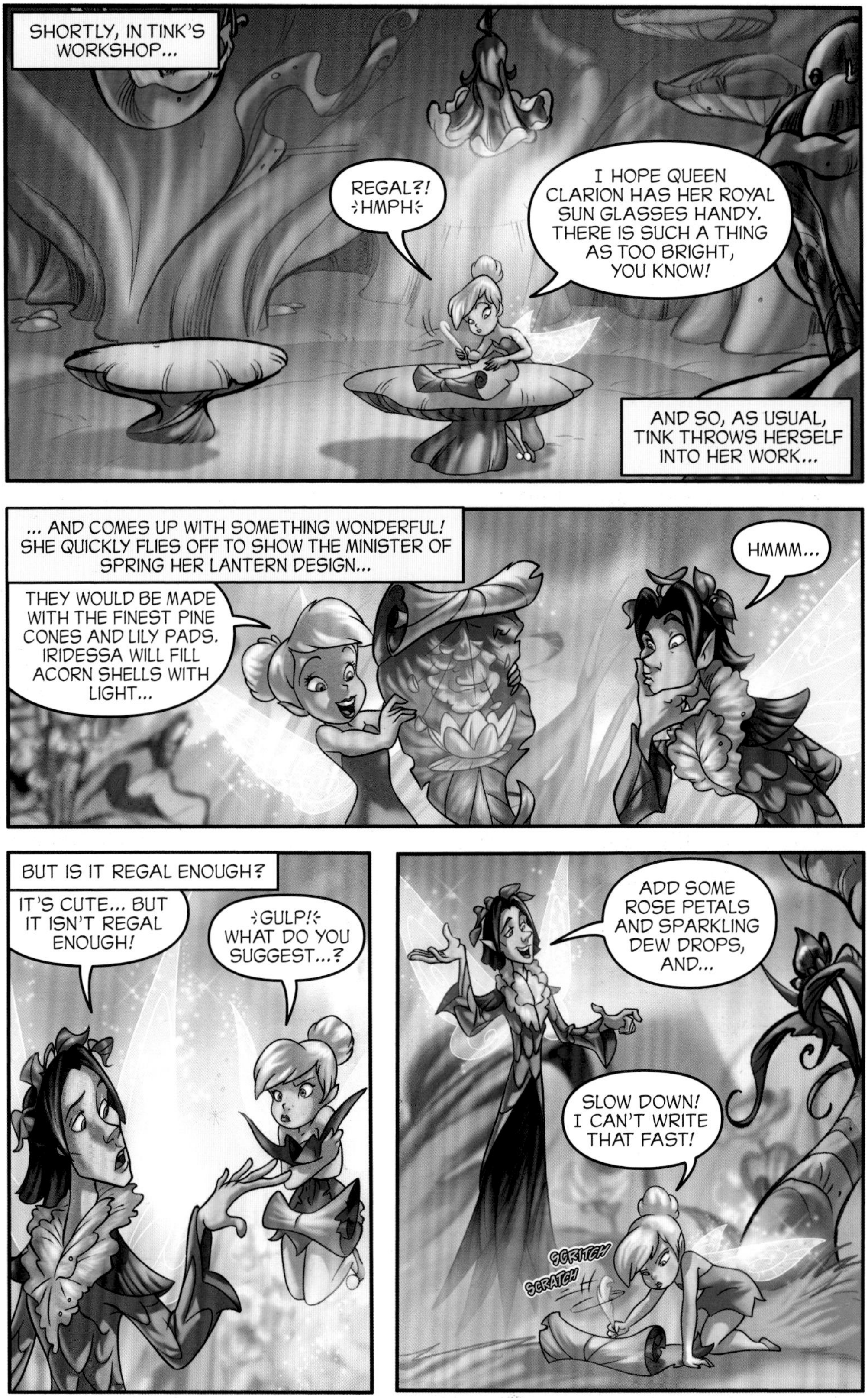
SHORTLY, IN TINK'S WORKSHOP...
REGAL?! ⁂HMPH⁂
I HOPE QUEEN CLARION HAS HER ROYAL SUN GLASSES HANDY. THERE IS SUCH A THING AS TOO BRIGHT, YOU KNOW!
AND SO, AS USUAL, TINK THROWS HERSELF INTO HER WORK...
... AND COMES UP WITH SOMETHING WONDERFUL! SHE QUICKLY FLIES OFF TO SHOW THE MINISTER OF SPRING HER LANTERN DESIGN...
THEY WOULD BE MADE WITH THE FINEST PINE CONES AND LILY PADS. IRIDESSA WILL FILL ACORN SHELLS WITH LIGHT...
HMMM...
BUT IS IT REGAL ENOUGH?
IT'S CUTE... BUT IT ISN'T REGAL ENOUGH!
⁂GULP!⁂ WHAT DO YOU SUGGEST...?
ADD SOME ROSE PETALS AND SPARKLING DEW DROPS, AND...
SLOW DOWN! I CAN'T WRITE THAT FAST!
SCRITCH
SCRATCH

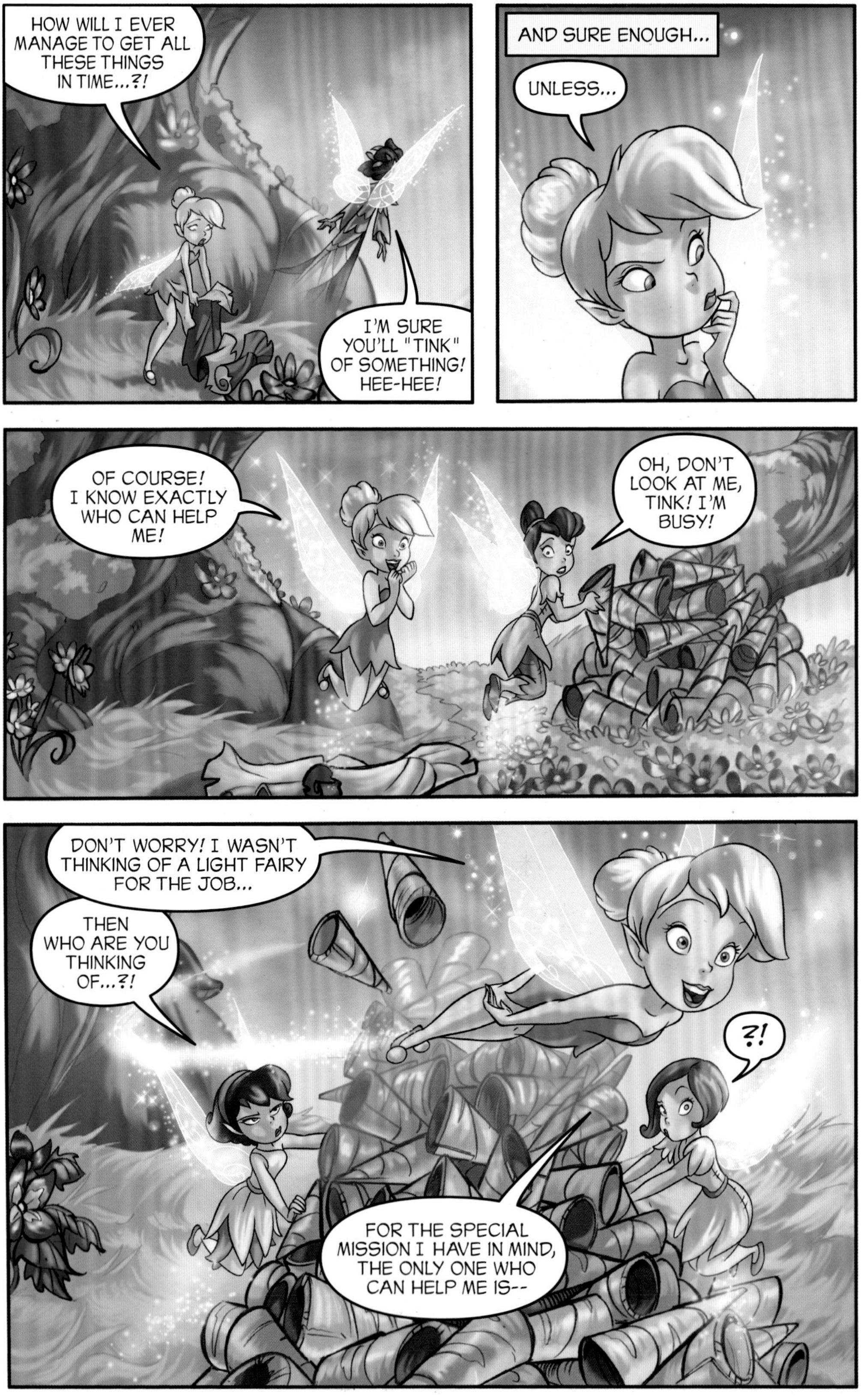
HOW WILL I EVER MANAGE TO GET ALL THESE THINGS IN TIME...?!
I'M SURE YOU'LL "TINK" OF SOMETHING! HEE-HEE!
AND SURE ENOUGH...
UNLESS...
OF COURSE! I KNOW EXACTLY WHO CAN HELP ME!
OH, DON'T LOOK AT ME, TINK! I'M BUSY!
DON'T WORRY! I WASN'T THINKING OF A LIGHT FAIRY FOR THE JOB...
THEN WHO ARE YOU THINKING OF...?!
?!
FOR THE SPECIAL MISSION I HAVE IN MIND, THE ONLY ONE WHO CAN HELP ME IS--

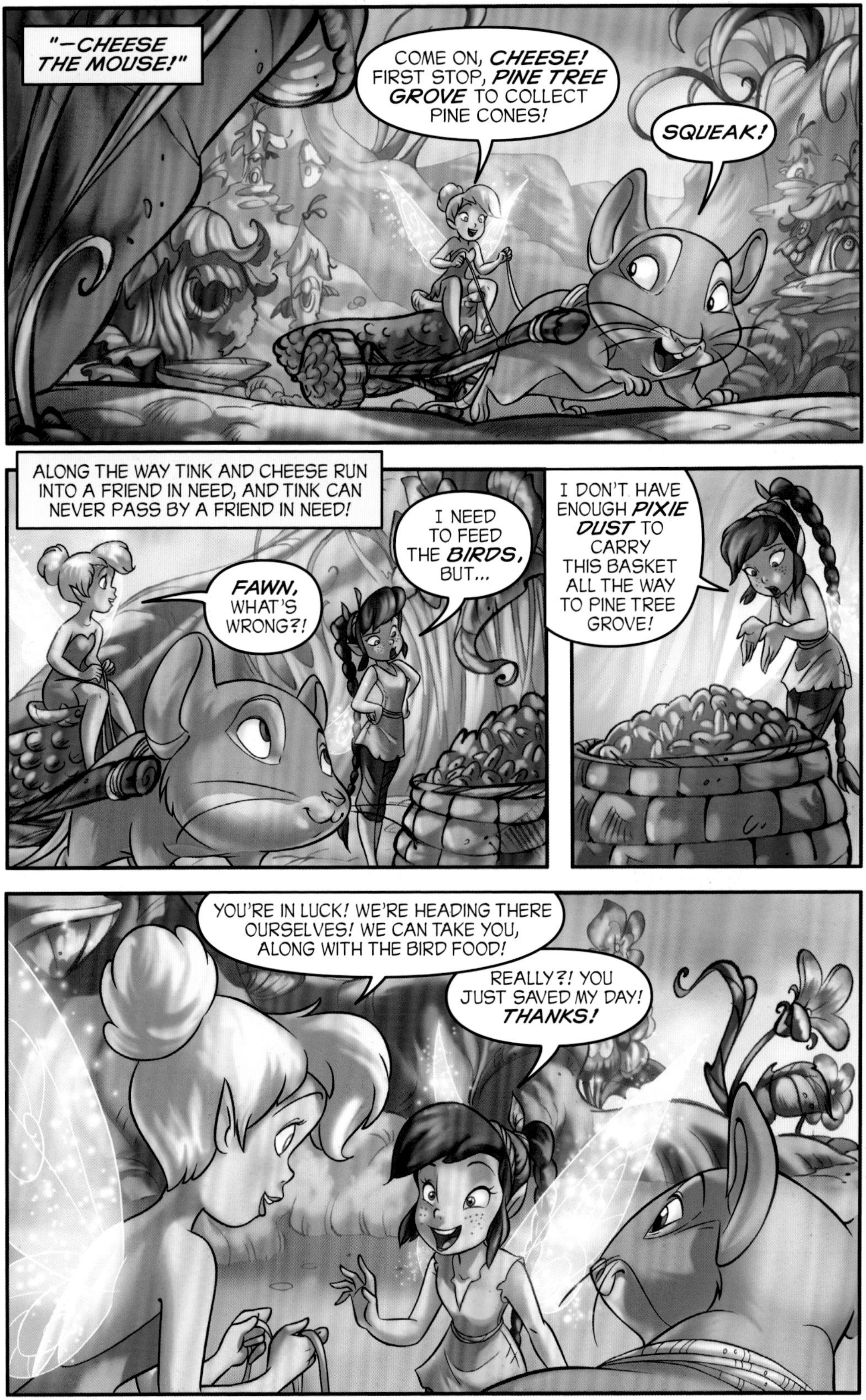
"—CHEESE THE MOUSE!"
COME ON, CHEESE! FIRST STOP, PINE TREE GROVE TO COLLECT PINE CONES!
SQUEAK!
ALONG THE WAY TINK AND CHEESE RUN INTO A FRIEND IN NEED, AND TINK CAN NEVER PASS BY A FRIEND IN NEED!
FAWN, WHAT'S WRONG?!
I NEED TO FEED THE BIRDS, BUT...
I DON'T HAVE ENOUGH PIXIE DUST TO CARRY THIS BASKET ALL THE WAY TO PINE TREE GROVE!
YOU'RE IN LUCK! WE'RE HEADING THERE OURSELVES! WE CAN TAKE YOU, ALONG WITH THE BIRD FOOD!
REALLY?! YOU JUST SAVED MY DAY! THANKS!

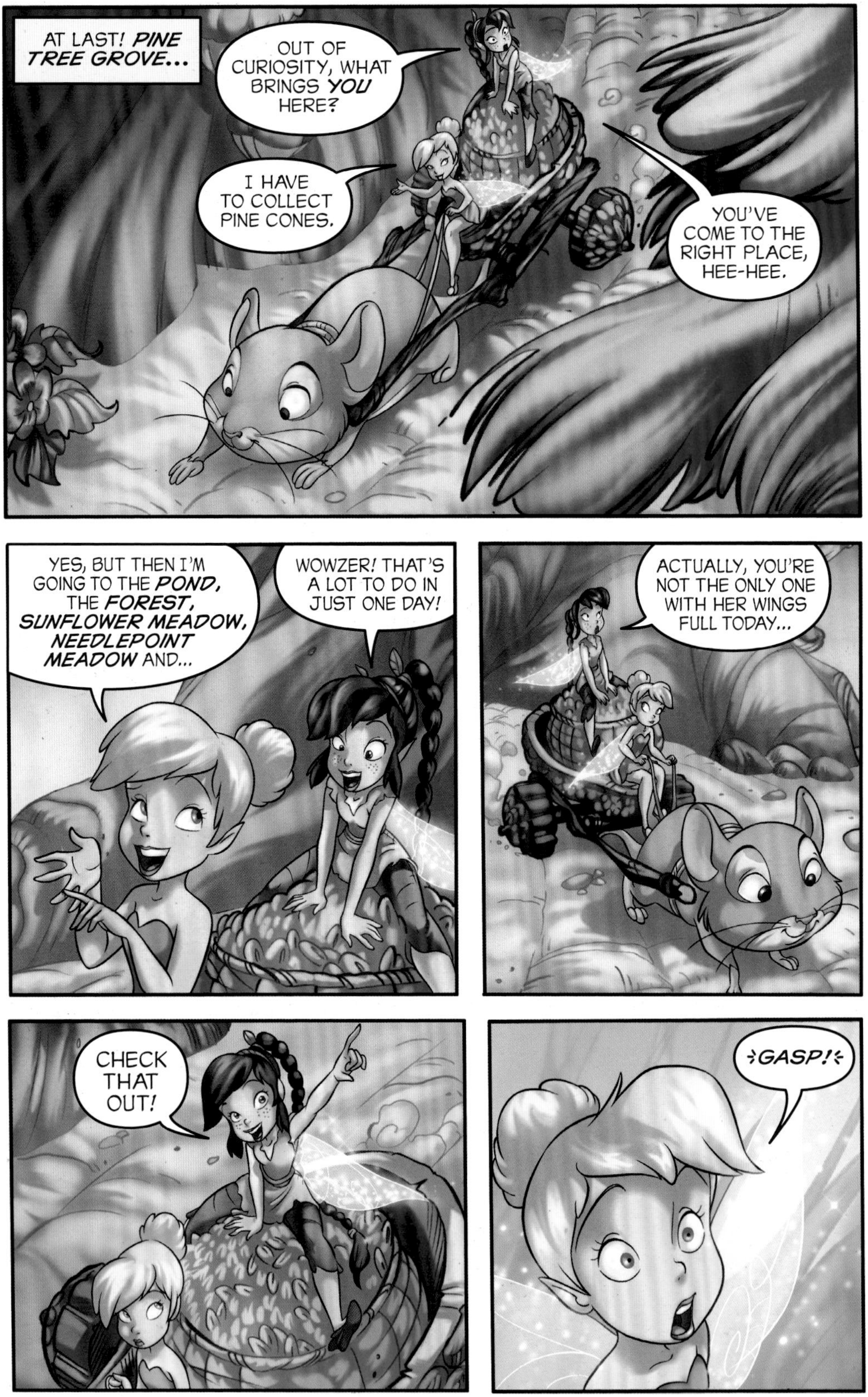
AT LAST! PINE TREE GROVE...
OUT OF CURIOSITY, WHAT BRINGS YOU HERE?
I HAVE TO COLLECT PINE CONES.
YOU'VE COME TO THE RIGHT PLACE, HEE-HEE.
YES, BUT THEN I'M GOING TO THE POND, THE FOREST, SUNFLOWER MEADOW, NEEDLEPOINT MEADOW AND...
WOWZER! THAT'S A LOT TO DO IN JUST ONE DAY!
ACTUALLY, YOU'RE NOT THE ONLY ONE WITH HER WINGS FULL TODAY...
CHECK THAT OUT!
GASP!

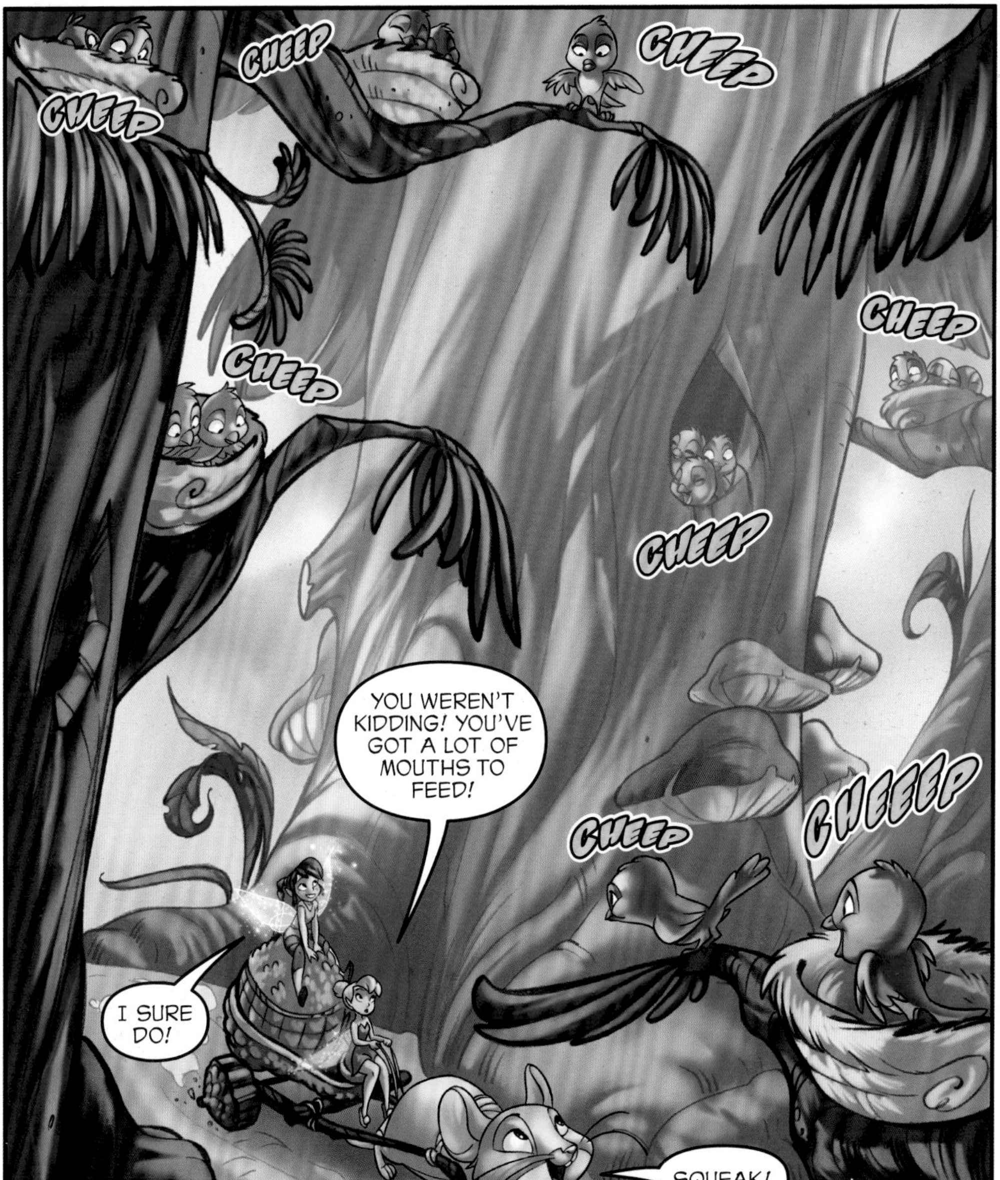
CHEEP
CHEEP
CHEEP
CHEEP
CHEEP
CHEEP
YOU WEREN'T KIDDING! YOU'VE GOT A LOT OF MOUTHS TO FEED!
I SURE DO!
CHEEP
CHEEEP
SQUEAK!

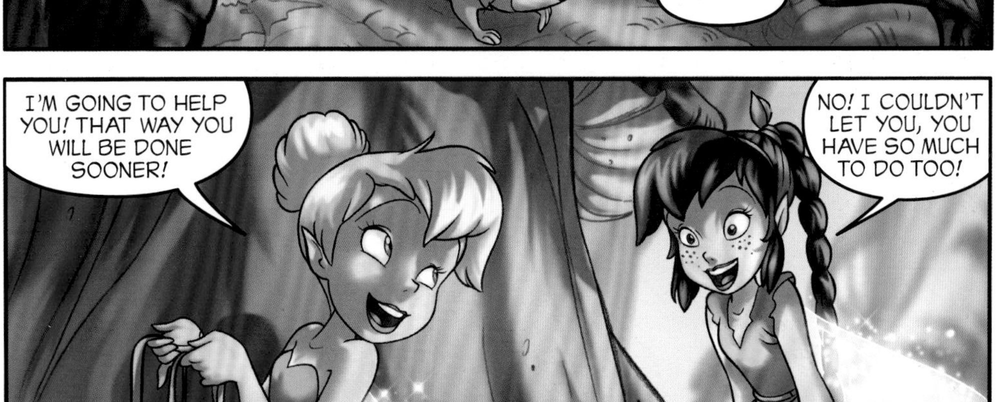
I'M GOING TO HELP YOU! THAT WAY YOU WILL BE DONE SOONER!
NO! I COULDN'T LET YOU, YOU HAVE SO MUCH TO DO TOO!

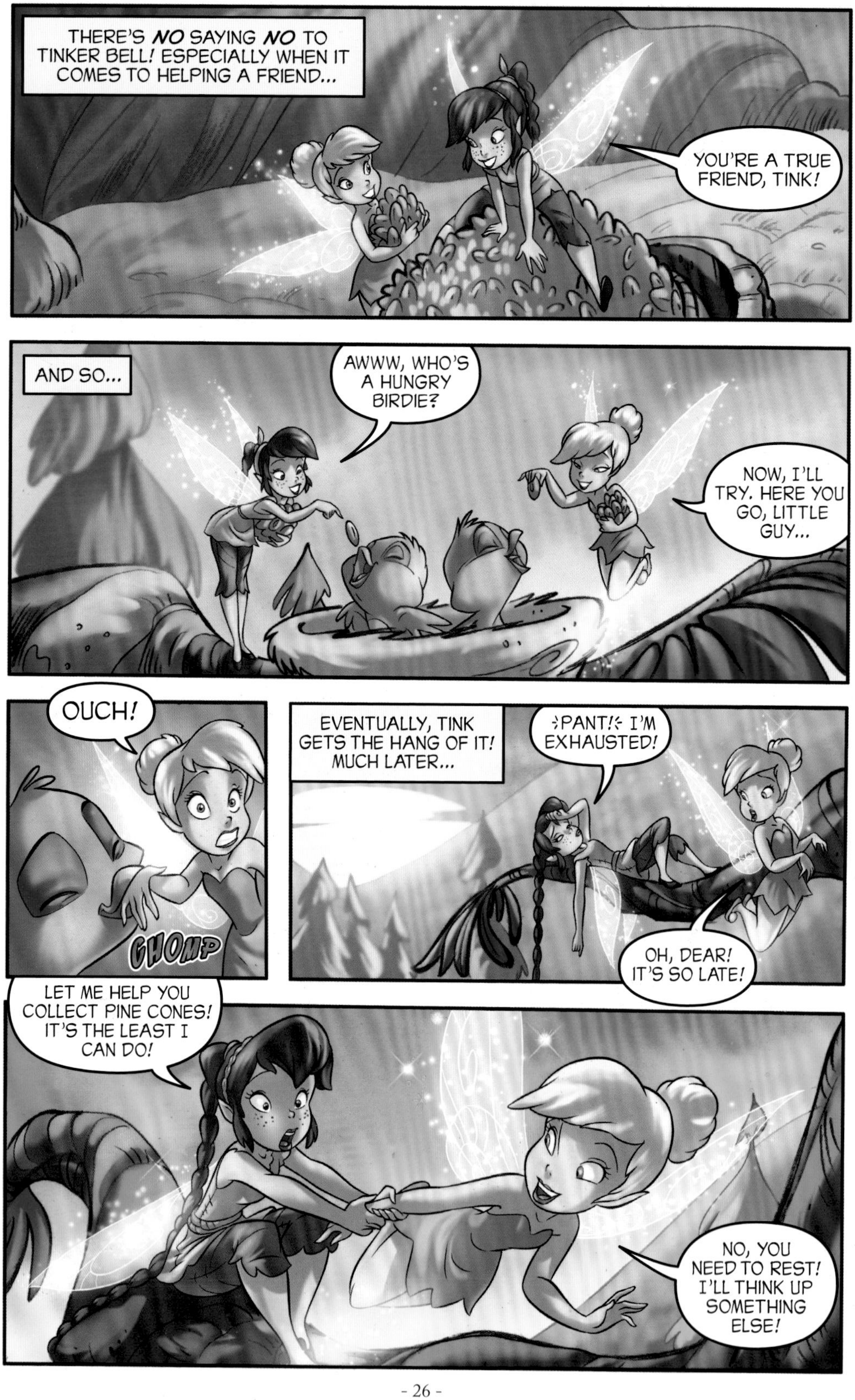
THERE'S NO SAYING NO TO TINKER BELL! ESPECIALLY WHEN IT COMES TO HELPING A FRIEND...
YOU'RE A TRUE FRIEND, TINK!
AND SO...
AWWW, WHO'S A HUNGRY BIRDIE?
NOW, I'LL TRY. HERE YOU GO, LITTLE GUY...
OUCH!
CHOMP
EVENTUALLY, TINK GETS THE HANG OF IT! MUCH LATER...
PANT! I'M EXHAUSTED!
OH, DEAR! IT'S SO LATE!
LET ME HELP YOU COLLECT PINE CONES! IT'S THE LEAST I CAN DO!
NO, YOU NEED TO REST! I'LL THINK UP SOMETHING ELSE!

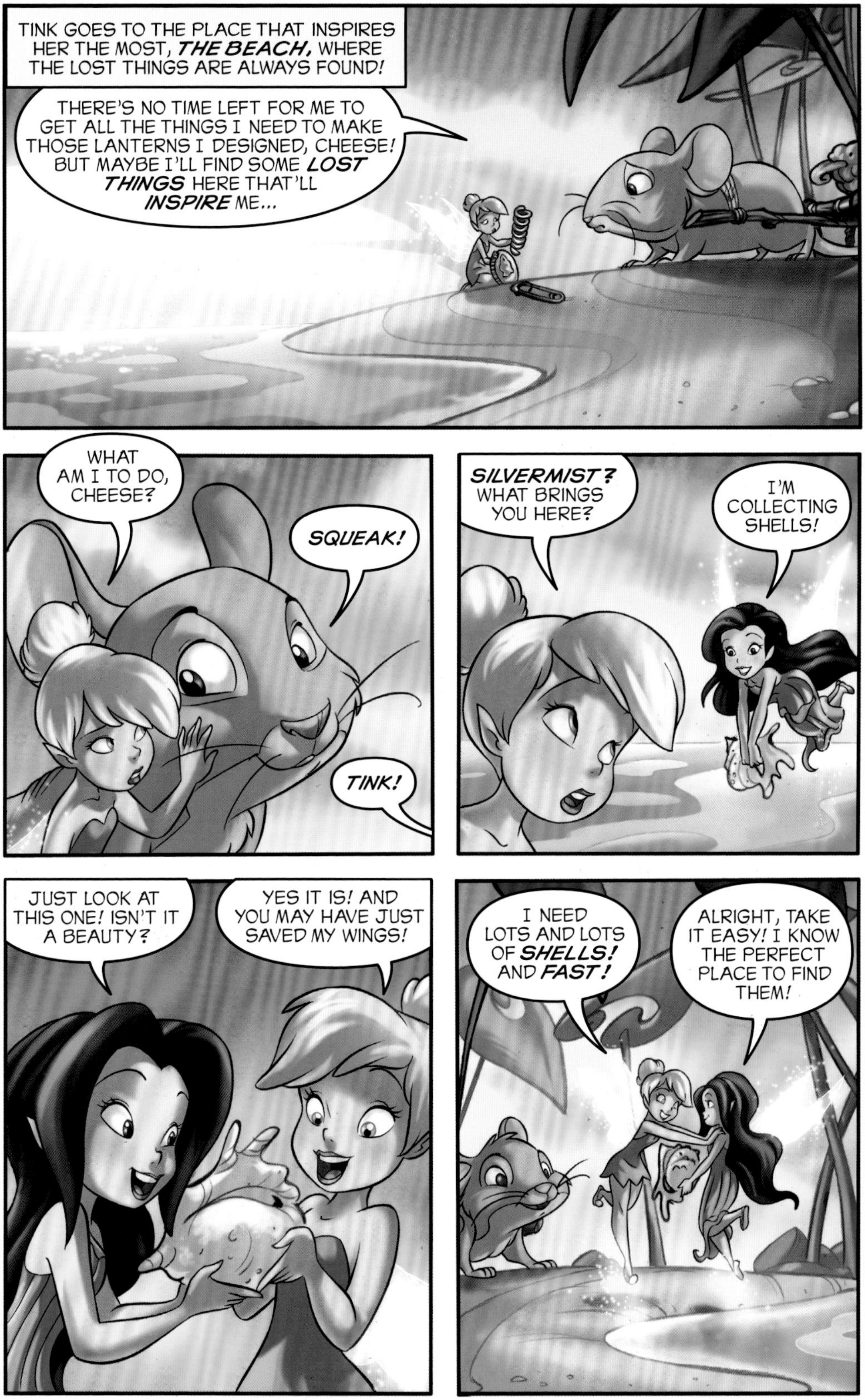
TINK GOES TO THE PLACE THAT INSPIRES HER THE MOST, ***THE BEACH,*** WHERE THE LOST THINGS ARE ALWAYS FOUND!
THERE'S NO TIME LEFT FOR ME TO GET ALL THE THINGS I NEED TO MAKE THOSE LANTERNS I DESIGNED, CHEESE! BUT MAYBE I'LL FIND SOME ***LOST THINGS*** HERE THAT'LL ***INSPIRE*** ME...
WHAT AM I TO DO, CHEESE?
SQUEAK!
TINK!
SILVERMIST? WHAT BRINGS YOU HERE?
I'M COLLECTING SHELLS!
JUST LOOK AT THIS ONE! ISN'T IT A BEAUTY?
YES IT IS! AND YOU MAY HAVE JUST SAVED MY WINGS!
I NEED LOTS AND LOTS OF ***SHELLS!*** AND ***FAST!***
ALRIGHT, TAKE IT EASY! I KNOW THE PERFECT PLACE TO FIND THEM!

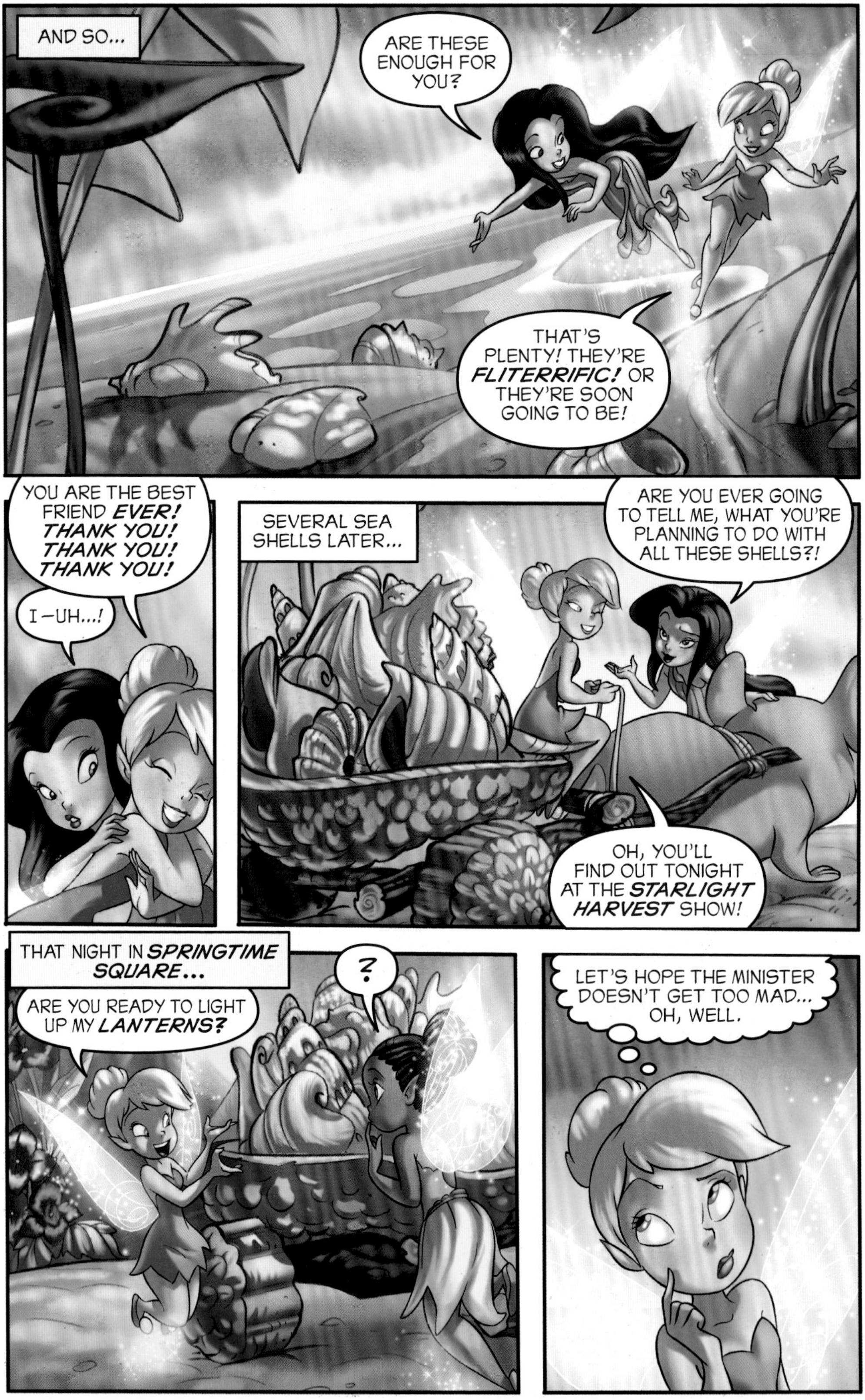
AND SO...
ARE THESE ENOUGH FOR YOU?
THAT'S PLENTY! THEY'RE FLITERRIFIC! OR THEY'RE SOON GOING TO BE!
YOU ARE THE BEST FRIEND EVER! THANK YOU! THANK YOU! THANK YOU!
I—UH...!
SEVERAL SEA SHELLS LATER...
ARE YOU EVER GOING TO TELL ME, WHAT YOU'RE PLANNING TO DO WITH ALL THESE SHELLS?!
OH, YOU'LL FIND OUT TONIGHT AT THE STARLIGHT HARVEST SHOW!
THAT NIGHT IN SPRINGTIME SQUARE...
ARE YOU READY TO LIGHT UP MY LANTERNS?
?
LET'S HOPE THE MINISTER DOESN'T GET TOO MAD... OH, WELL.

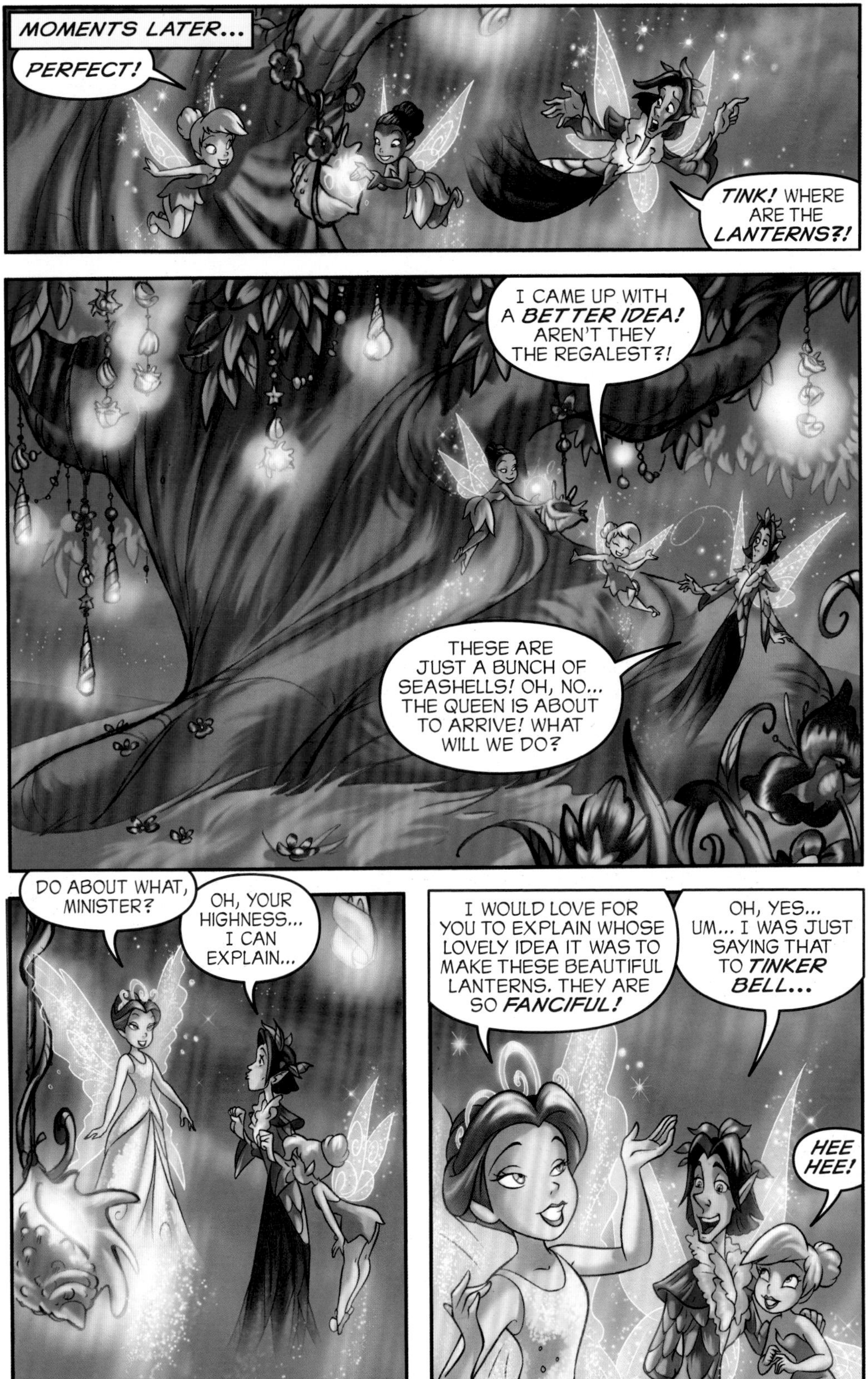
MOMENTS LATER...
PERFECT!
TINK! WHERE ARE THE LANTERNS?!
I CAME UP WITH A BETTER IDEA! AREN'T THEY THE REGALEST?!
THESE ARE JUST A BUNCH OF SEASHELLS! OH, NO... THE QUEEN IS ABOUT TO ARRIVE! WHAT WILL WE DO?
DO ABOUT WHAT, MINISTER?
OH, YOUR HIGHNESS... I CAN EXPLAIN...
I WOULD LOVE FOR YOU TO EXPLAIN WHOSE LOVELY IDEA IT WAS TO MAKE THESE BEAUTIFUL LANTERNS. THEY ARE SO FANCIFUL!
OH, YES... UM... I WAS JUST SAYING THAT TO TINKER BELL...
HEE HEE!

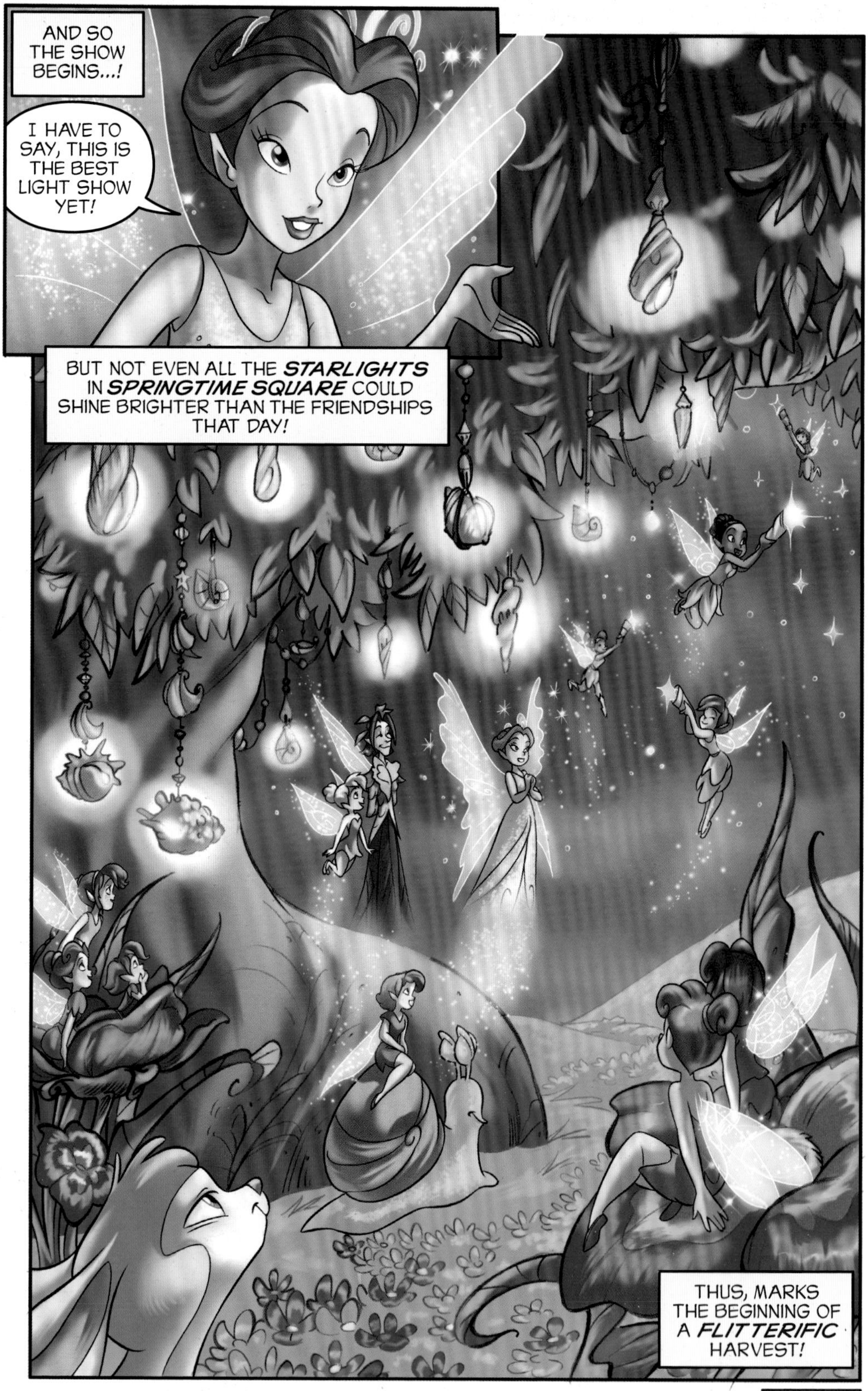
AND SO THE SHOW BEGINS...!
I HAVE TO SAY, THIS IS THE BEST LIGHT SHOW YET!
BUT NOT EVEN ALL THE STARLIGHTS IN SPRINGTIME SQUARE COULD SHINE BRIGHTER THAN THE FRIENDSHIPS THAT DAY!
THUS, MARKS THE BEGINNING OF A FLITTERIFIC HARVEST!

THE END

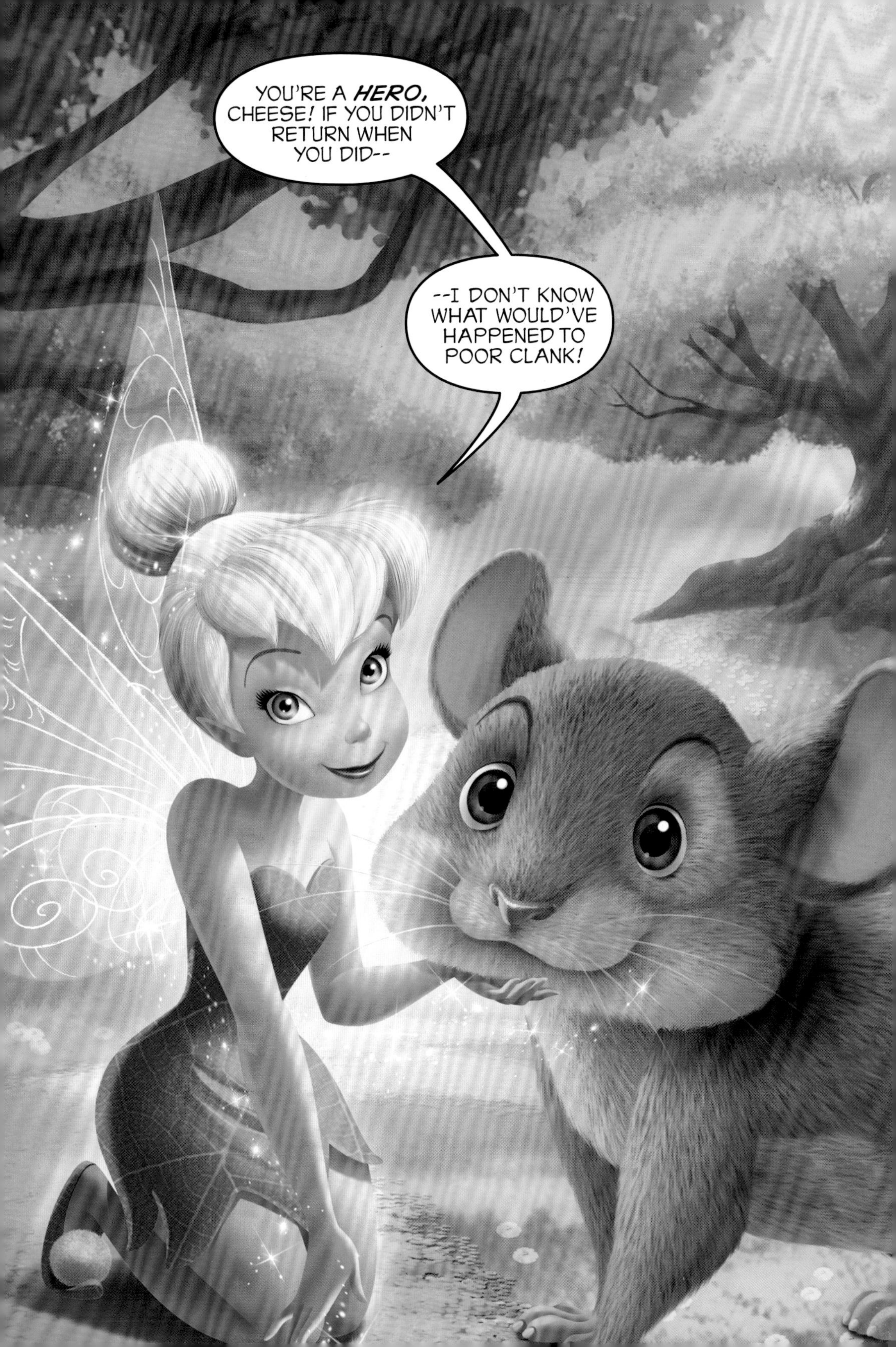
YOU'RE A *HERO,* CHEESE! IF YOU DIDN'T RETURN WHEN YOU DID--
--I DON'T KNOW WHAT WOULD'VE HAPPENED TO POOR CLANK!

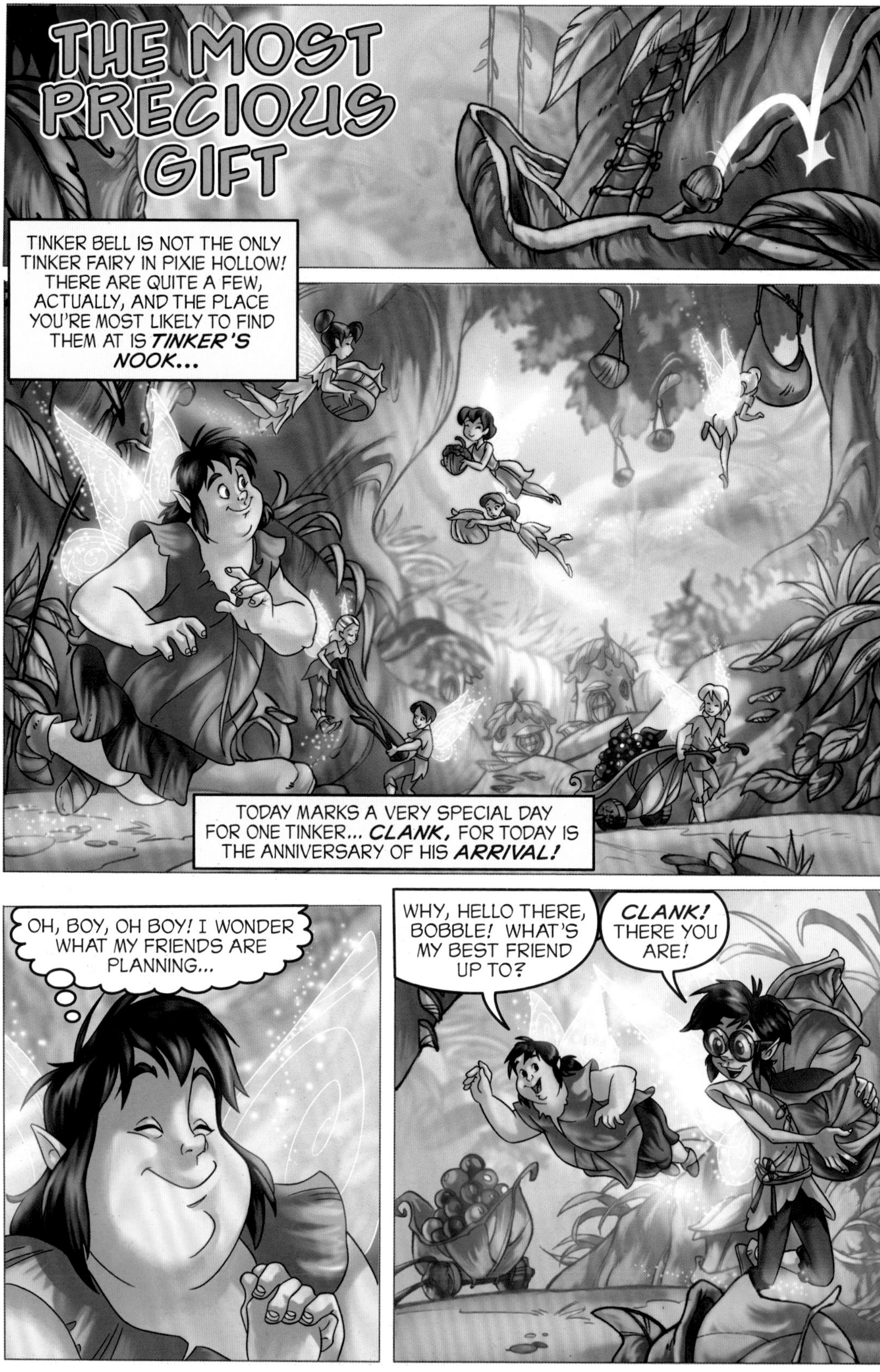
THE MOST PRECIOUS GIFT
TINKER BELL IS NOT THE ONLY TINKER FAIRY IN PIXIE HOLLOW! THERE ARE QUITE A FEW, ACTUALLY, AND THE PLACE YOU'RE MOST LIKELY TO FIND THEM AT IS *TINKER'S NOOK...*
TODAY MARKS A VERY SPECIAL DAY FOR ONE TINKER... *CLANK,* FOR TODAY IS THE ANNIVERSARY OF HIS *ARRIVAL!*
OH, BOY, OH BOY! I WONDER WHAT MY FRIENDS ARE PLANNING...
CLANK! THERE YOU ARE!
WHY, HELLO THERE, BOBBLE! WHAT'S MY BEST FRIEND UP TO?

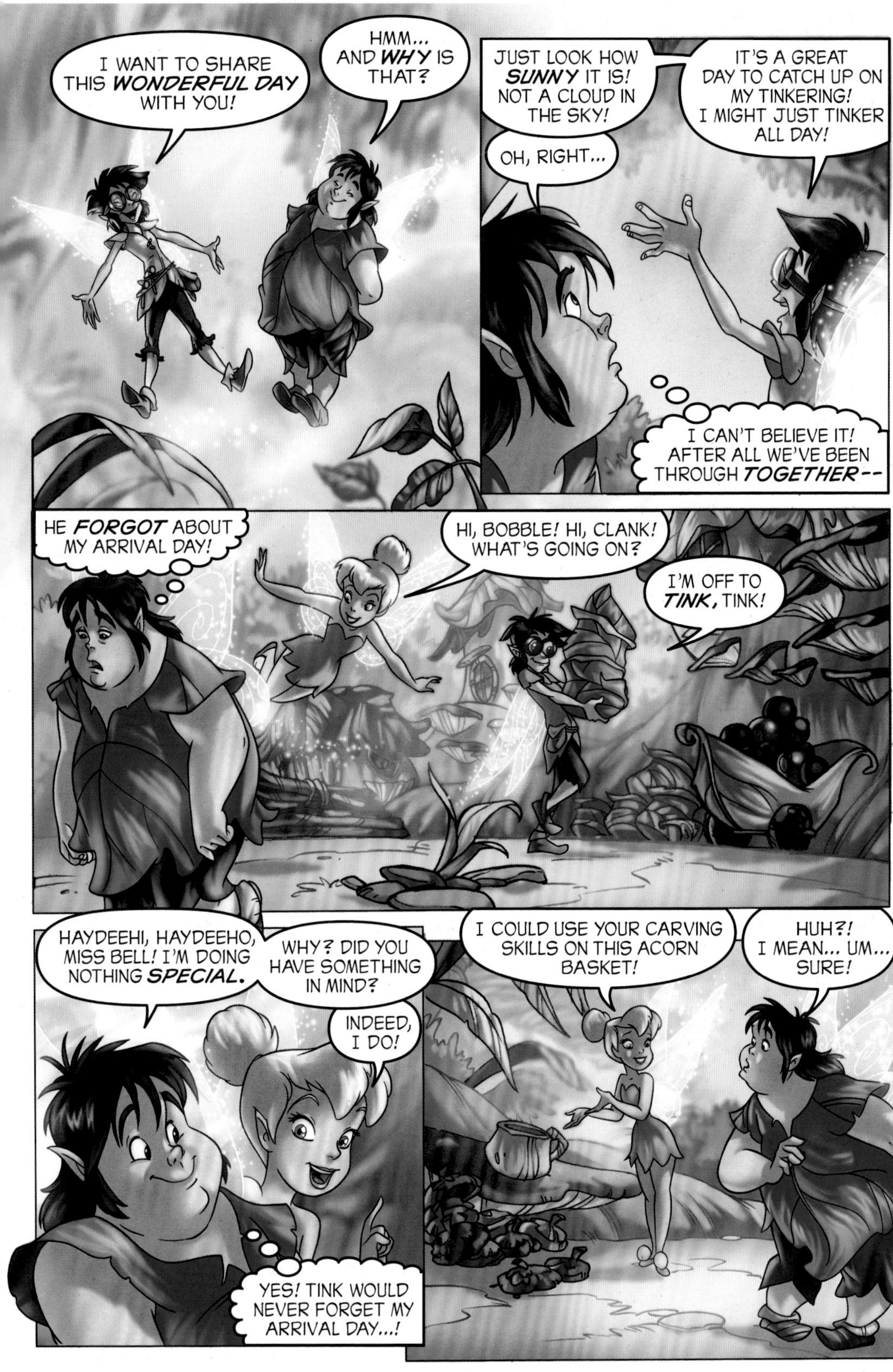
I WANT TO SHARE THIS WONDERFUL DAY WITH YOU!
HMM... AND WHY IS THAT?
JUST LOOK HOW SUNNY IT IS! NOT A CLOUD IN THE SKY!
IT'S A GREAT DAY TO CATCH UP ON MY TINKERING! I MIGHT JUST TINKER ALL DAY!
OH, RIGHT...
I CAN'T BELIEVE IT! AFTER ALL WE'VE BEEN THROUGH TOGETHER--
HE FORGOT ABOUT MY ARRIVAL DAY!
HI, BOBBLE! HI, CLANK! WHAT'S GOING ON?
I'M OFF TO TINK, TINK!
HAYDEEHI, HAYDEEHO, MISS BELL! I'M DOING NOTHING SPECIAL.
WHY? DID YOU HAVE SOMETHING IN MIND?
INDEED, I DO!
YES! TINK WOULD NEVER FORGET MY ARRIVAL DAY...!
I COULD USE YOUR CARVING SKILLS ON THIS ACORN BASKET!
HUH?! I MEAN... UM... SURE!

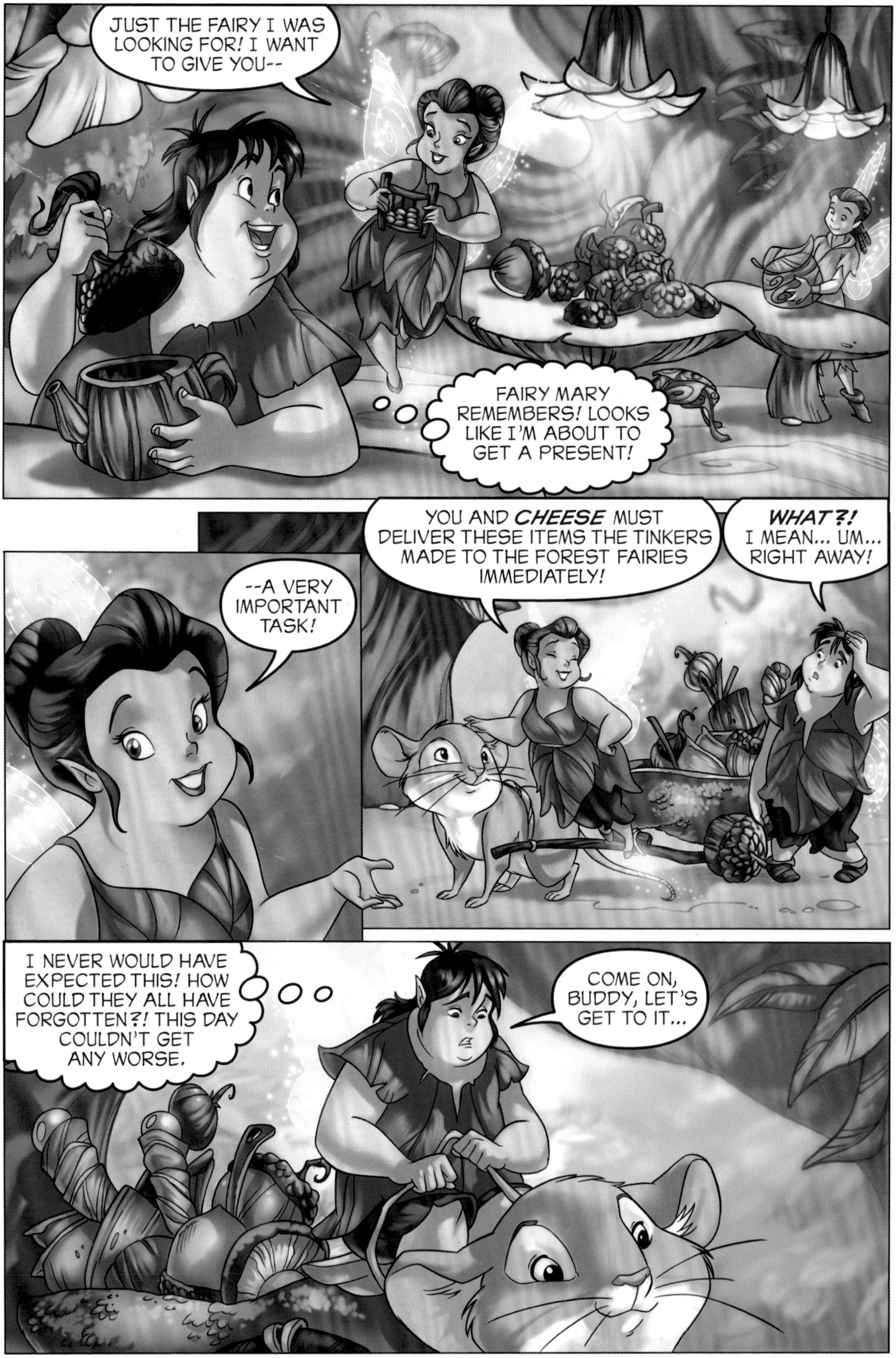
JUST THE FAIRY I WAS LOOKING FOR! I WANT TO GIVE YOU--
FAIRY MARY REMEMBERS! LOOKS LIKE I'M ABOUT TO GET A PRESENT!
--A VERY IMPORTANT TASK!
YOU AND *CHEESE* MUST DELIVER THESE ITEMS THE TINKERS MADE TO THE FOREST FAIRIES IMMEDIATELY!
WHAT?! I MEAN... UM... RIGHT AWAY!
I NEVER WOULD HAVE EXPECTED THIS! HOW COULD THEY ALL HAVE FORGOTTEN?! THIS DAY COULDN'T GET ANY WORSE.
COME ON, BUDDY, LET'S GET TO IT...

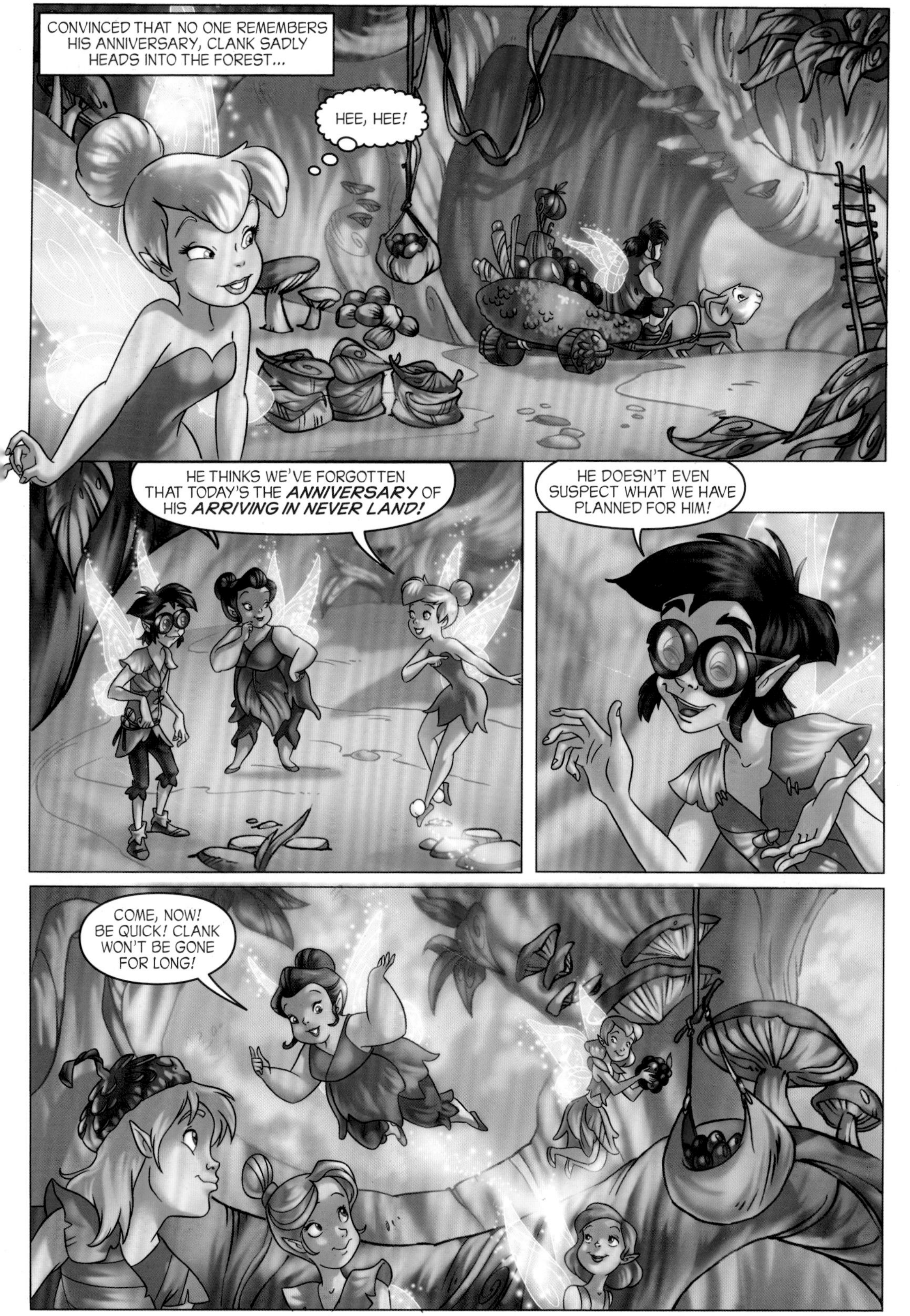
CONVINCED THAT NO ONE REMEMBERS HIS ANNIVERSARY, CLANK SADLY HEADS INTO THE FOREST...
HEE, HEE!
HE THINKS WE'VE FORGOTTEN THAT TODAY'S THE ***ANNIVERSARY*** OF HIS ***ARRIVING IN NEVER LAND!***
HE DOESN'T EVEN SUSPECT WHAT WE HAVE PLANNED FOR HIM!
COME, NOW! BE QUICK! CLANK WON'T BE GONE FOR LONG!

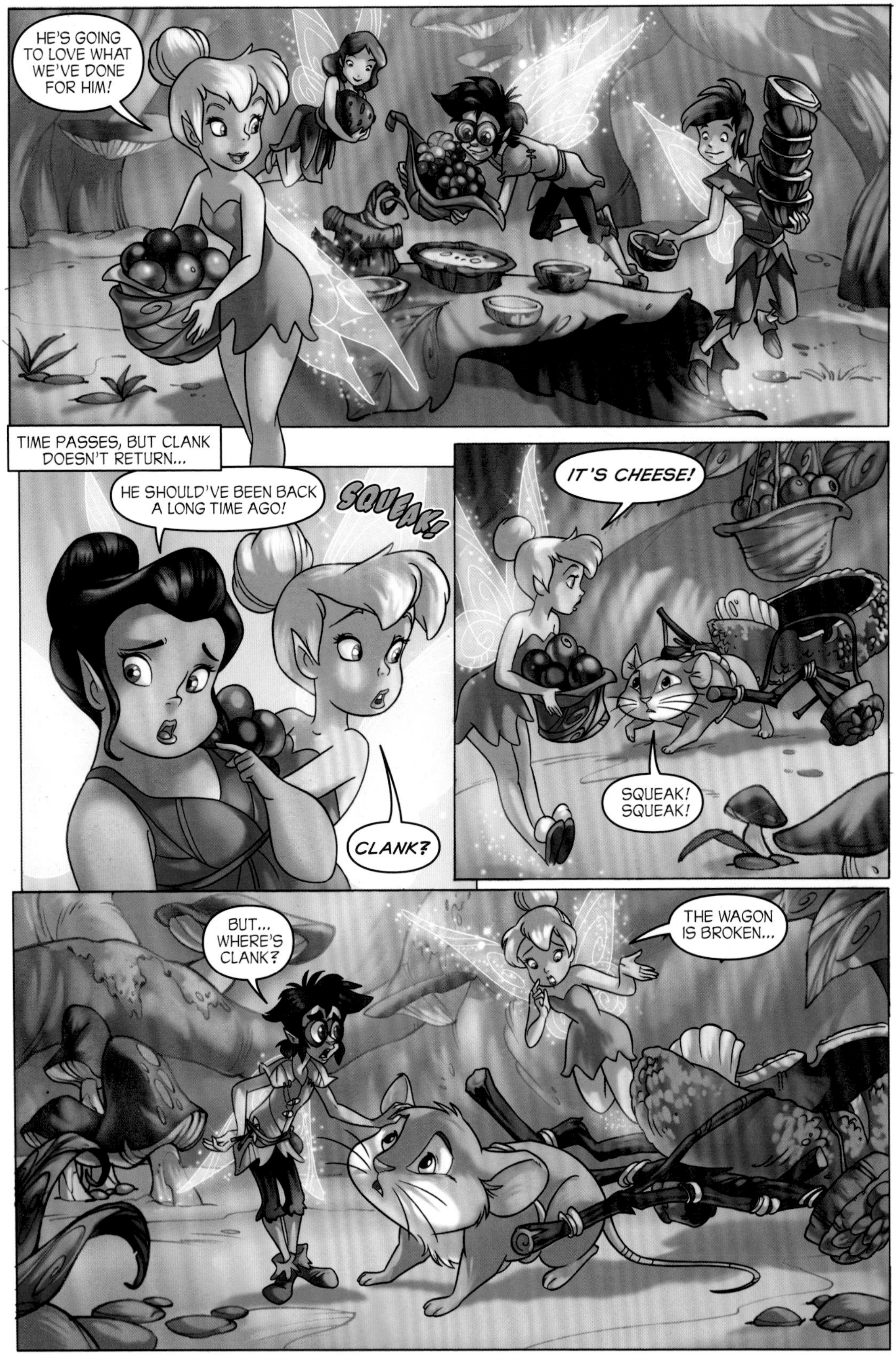
HE'S GOING TO LOVE WHAT WE'VE DONE FOR HIM!
TIME PASSES, BUT CLANK DOESN'T RETURN...
HE SHOULD'VE BEEN BACK A LONG TIME AGO!
SQUEAK!
CLANK?
IT'S CHEESE!
SQUEAK! SQUEAK!
BUT... WHERE'S CLANK?
THE WAGON IS BROKEN...

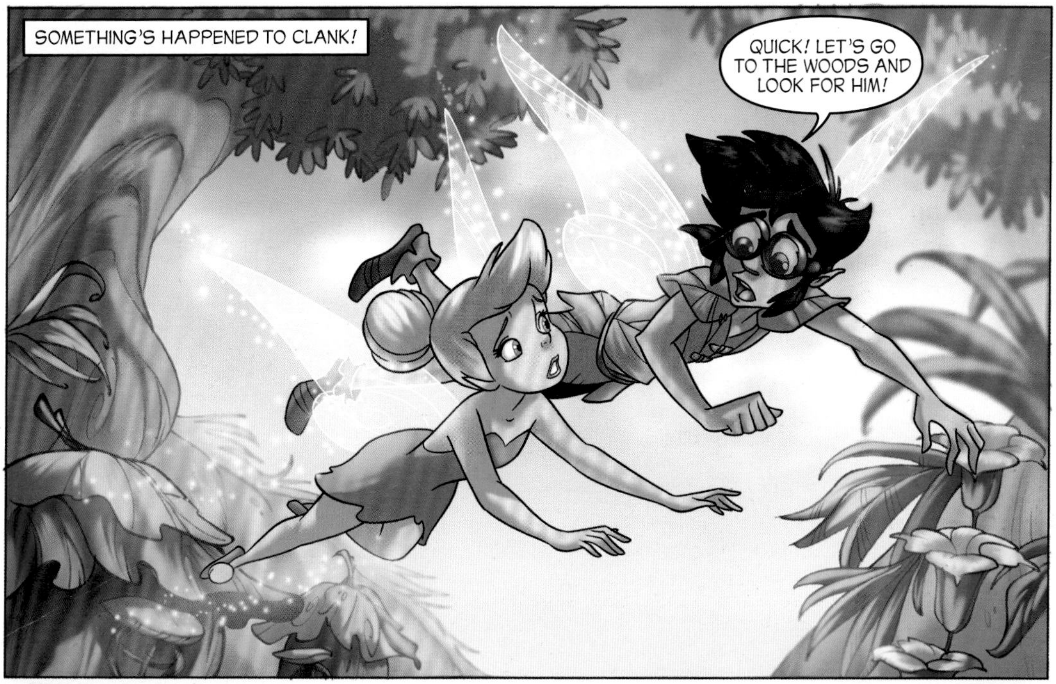
SOMETHING'S HAPPENED TO CLANK!
QUICK! LET'S GO TO THE WOODS AND LOOK FOR HIM!

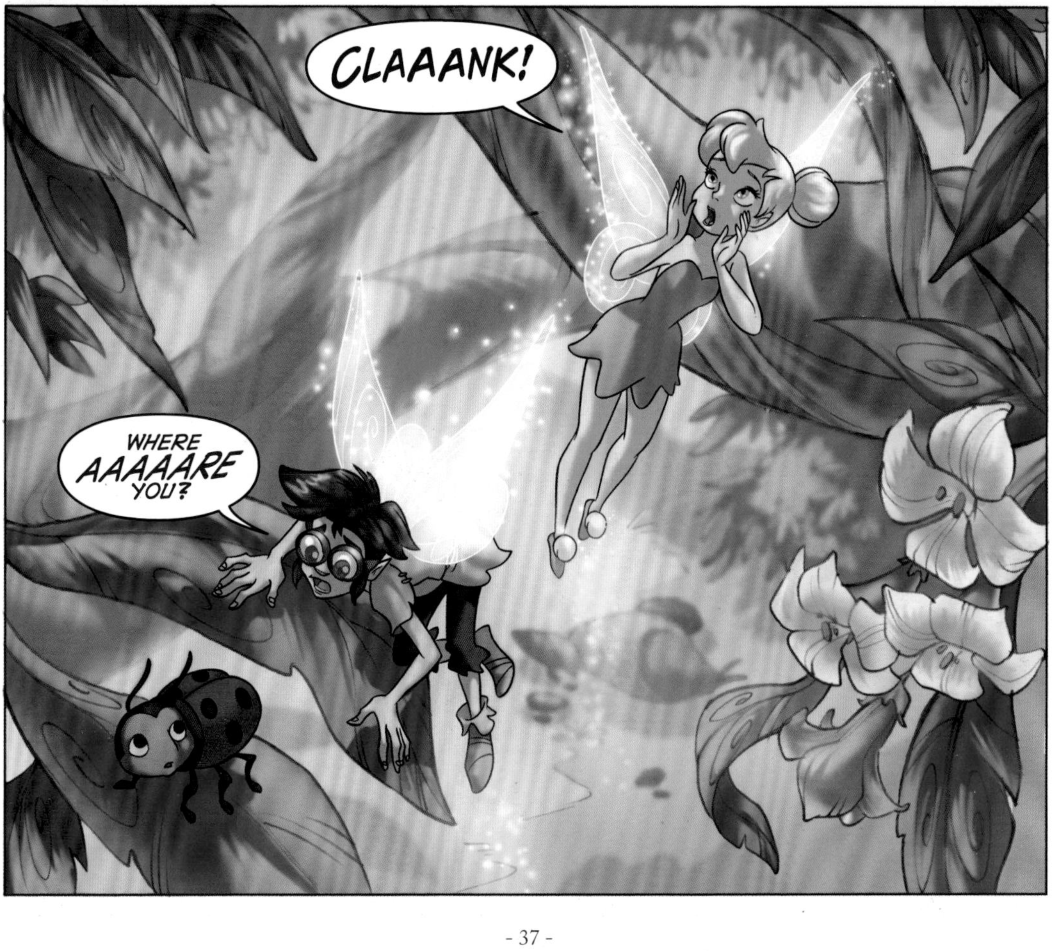
CLAAANK!
WHERE AAAAARE YOU?

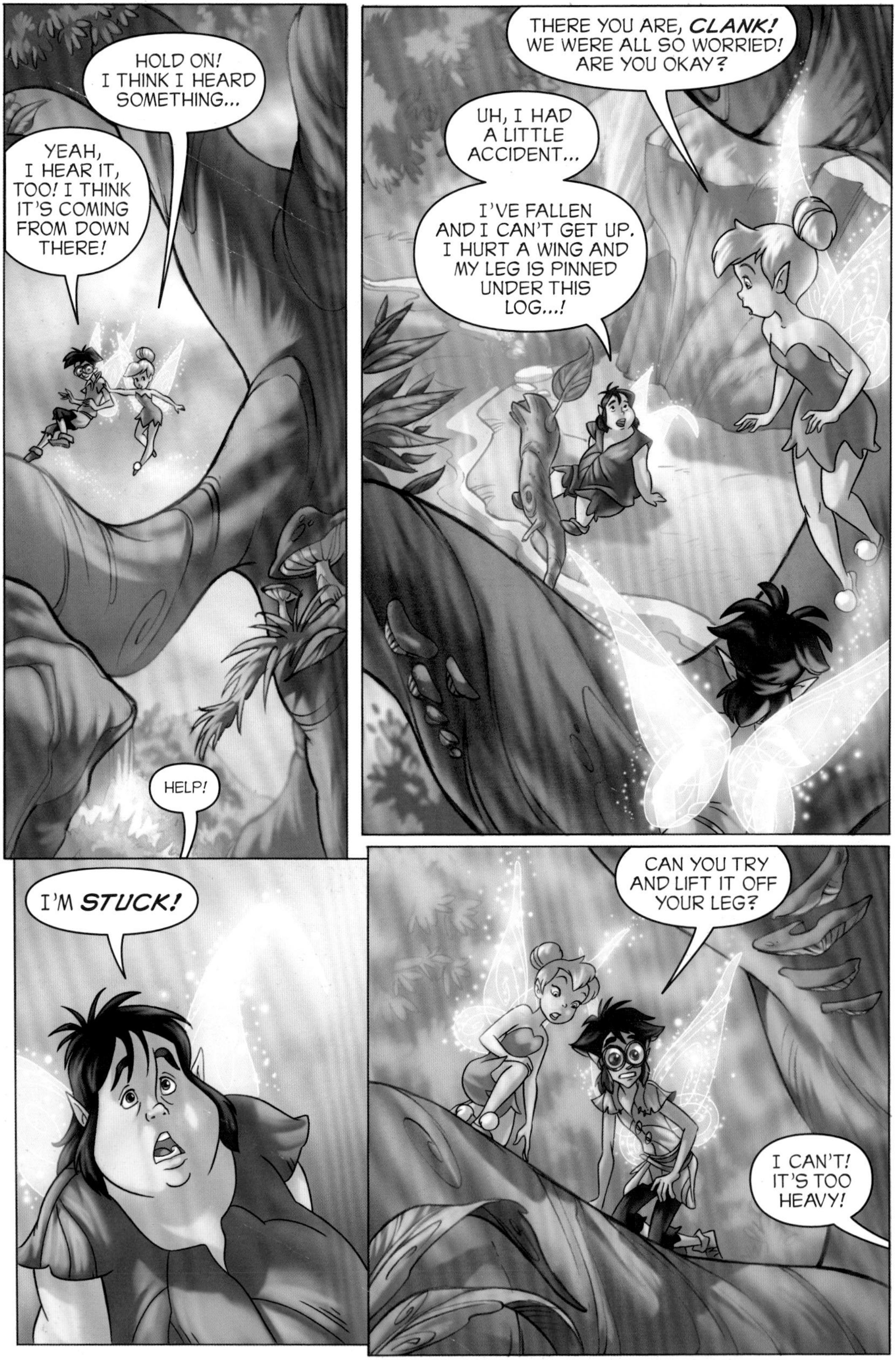
HOLD ON! I THINK I HEARD SOMETHING...
YEAH, I HEAR IT, TOO! I THINK IT'S COMING FROM DOWN THERE!
HELP!
I'M STUCK!
THERE YOU ARE, CLANK! WE WERE ALL SO WORRIED! ARE YOU OKAY?
UH, I HAD A LITTLE ACCIDENT...
I'VE FALLEN AND I CAN'T GET UP. I HURT A WING AND MY LEG IS PINNED UNDER THIS LOG...!
CAN YOU TRY AND LIFT IT OFF YOUR LEG?
I CAN'T! IT'S TOO HEAVY!

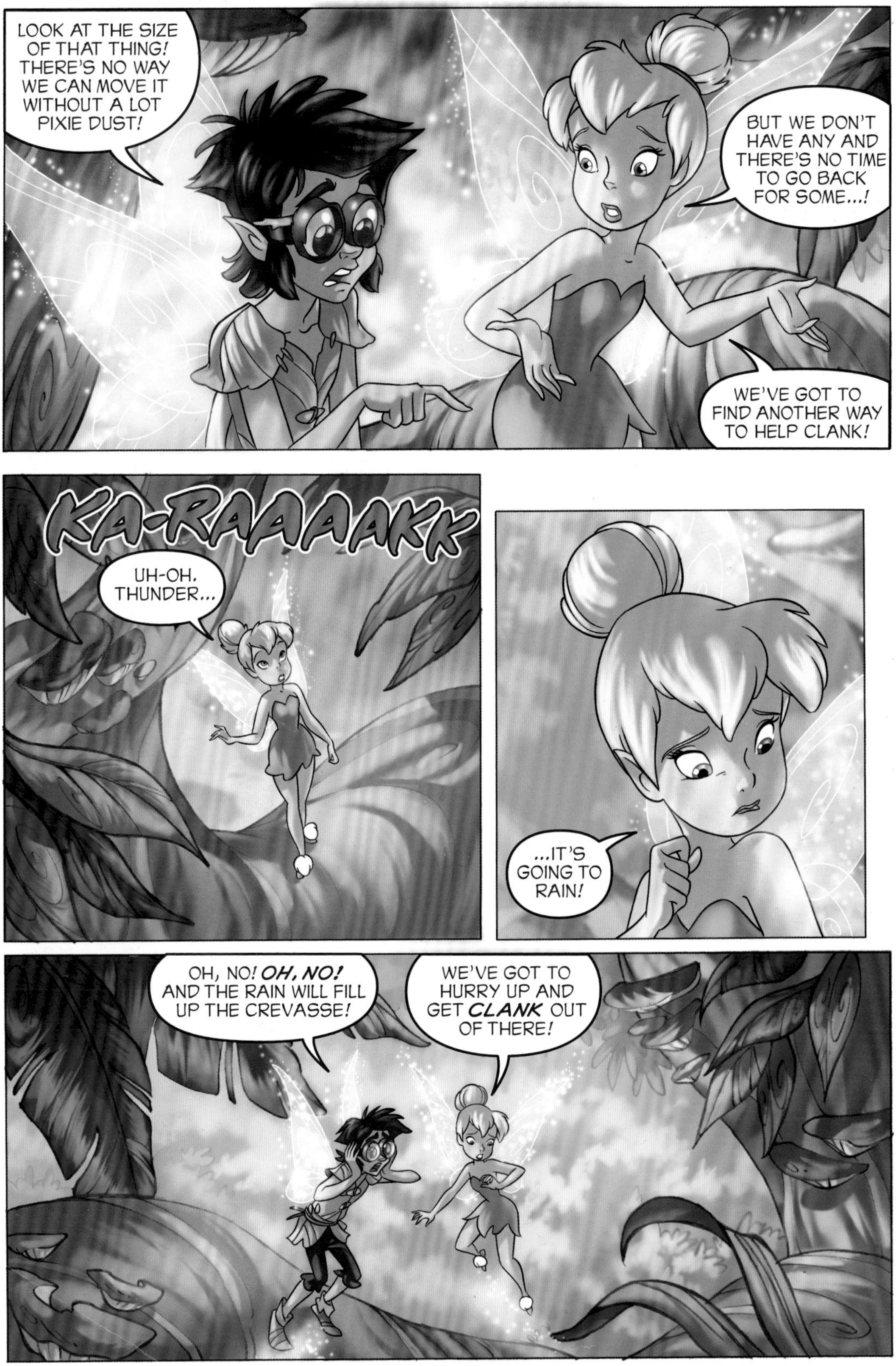
LOOK AT THE SIZE OF THAT THING! THERE'S NO WAY WE CAN MOVE IT WITHOUT A LOT PIXIE DUST!
BUT WE DON'T HAVE ANY AND THERE'S NO TIME TO GO BACK FOR SOME...!
WE'VE GOT TO FIND ANOTHER WAY TO HELP CLANK!
KA-RAAAAKK
UH-OH. THUNDER...
...IT'S GOING TO RAIN!
OH, NO! OH, NO! AND THE RAIN WILL FILL UP THE CREVASSE!
WE'VE GOT TO HURRY UP AND GET CLANK OUT OF THERE!

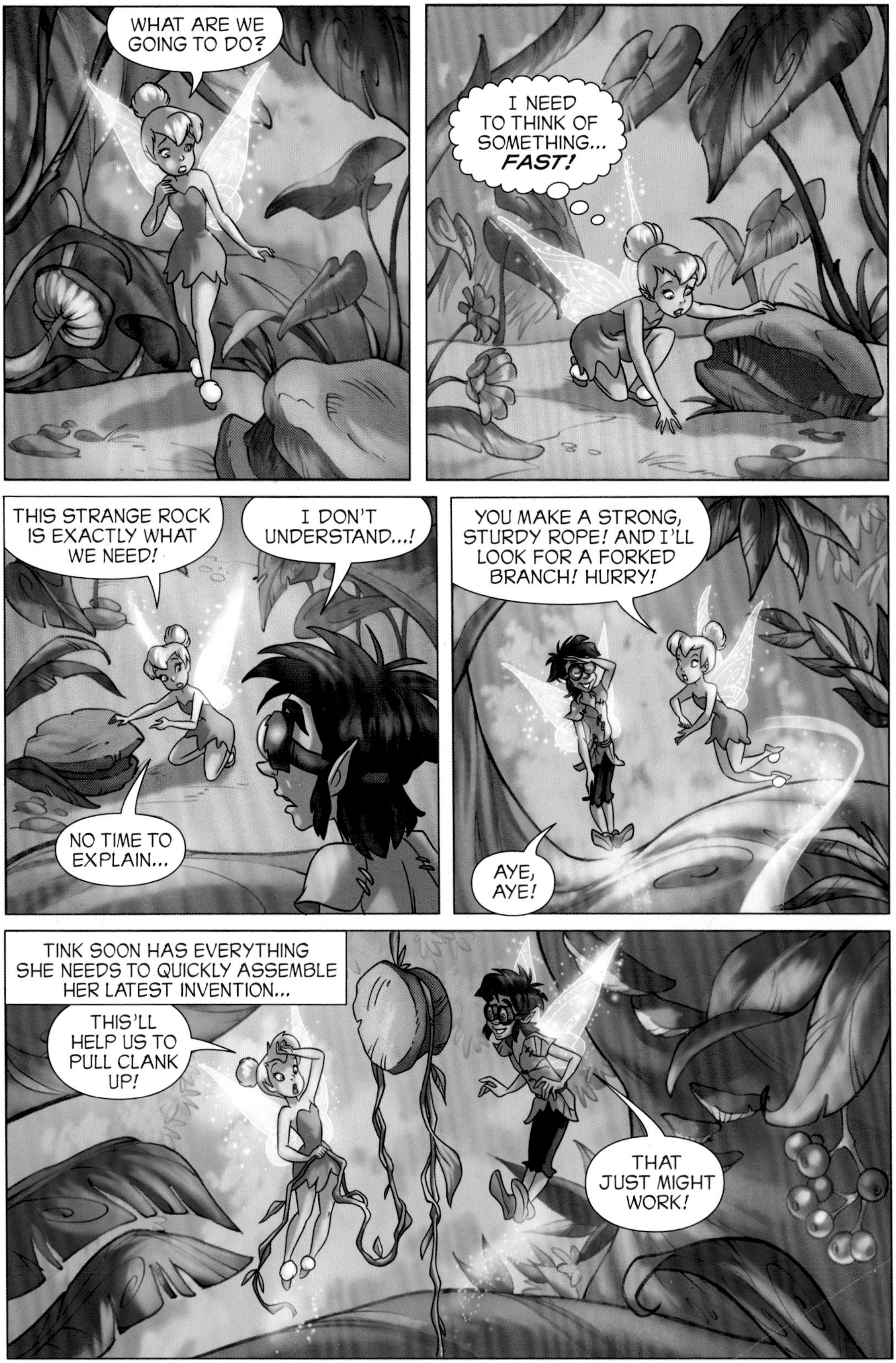
WHAT ARE WE GOING TO DO?
I NEED TO THINK OF SOMETHING... FAST!
THIS STRANGE ROCK IS EXACTLY WHAT WE NEED!
I DON'T UNDERSTAND...!
NO TIME TO EXPLAIN...
YOU MAKE A STRONG, STURDY ROPE! AND I'LL LOOK FOR A FORKED BRANCH! HURRY!
AYE, AYE!
TINK SOON HAS EVERYTHING SHE NEEDS TO QUICKLY ASSEMBLE HER LATEST INVENTION...
THIS'LL HELP US TO PULL CLANK UP!
THAT JUST MIGHT WORK!

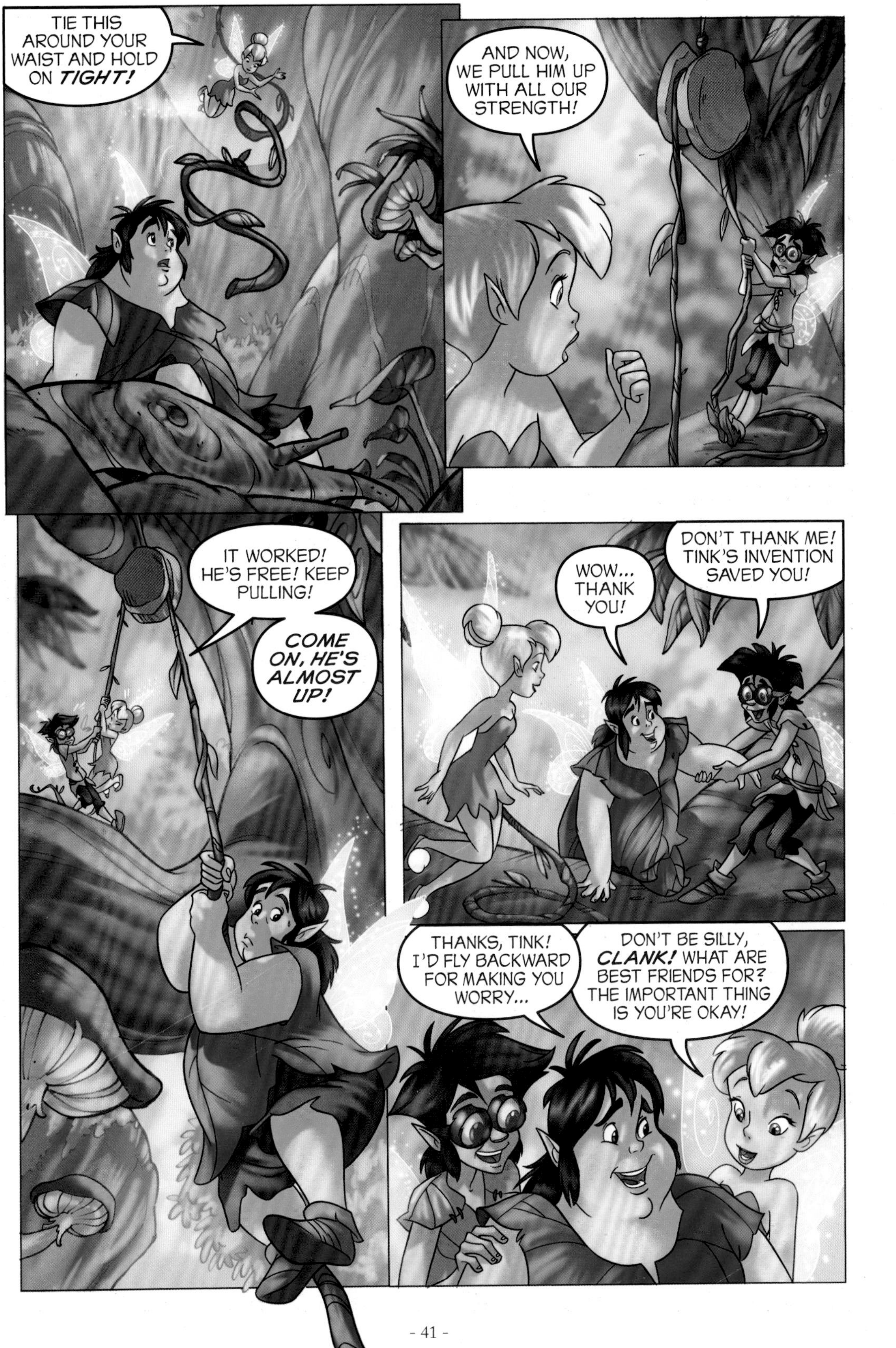
TIE THIS AROUND YOUR WAIST AND HOLD ON TIGHT!
AND NOW, WE PULL HIM UP WITH ALL OUR STRENGTH!
IT WORKED! HE'S FREE! KEEP PULLING!
COME ON, HE'S ALMOST UP!
WOW... THANK YOU!
DON'T THANK ME! TINK'S INVENTION SAVED YOU!
THANKS, TINK! I'D FLY BACKWARD FOR MAKING YOU WORRY...
DON'T BE SILLY, CLANK! WHAT ARE BEST FRIENDS FOR? THE IMPORTANT THING IS YOU'RE OKAY!

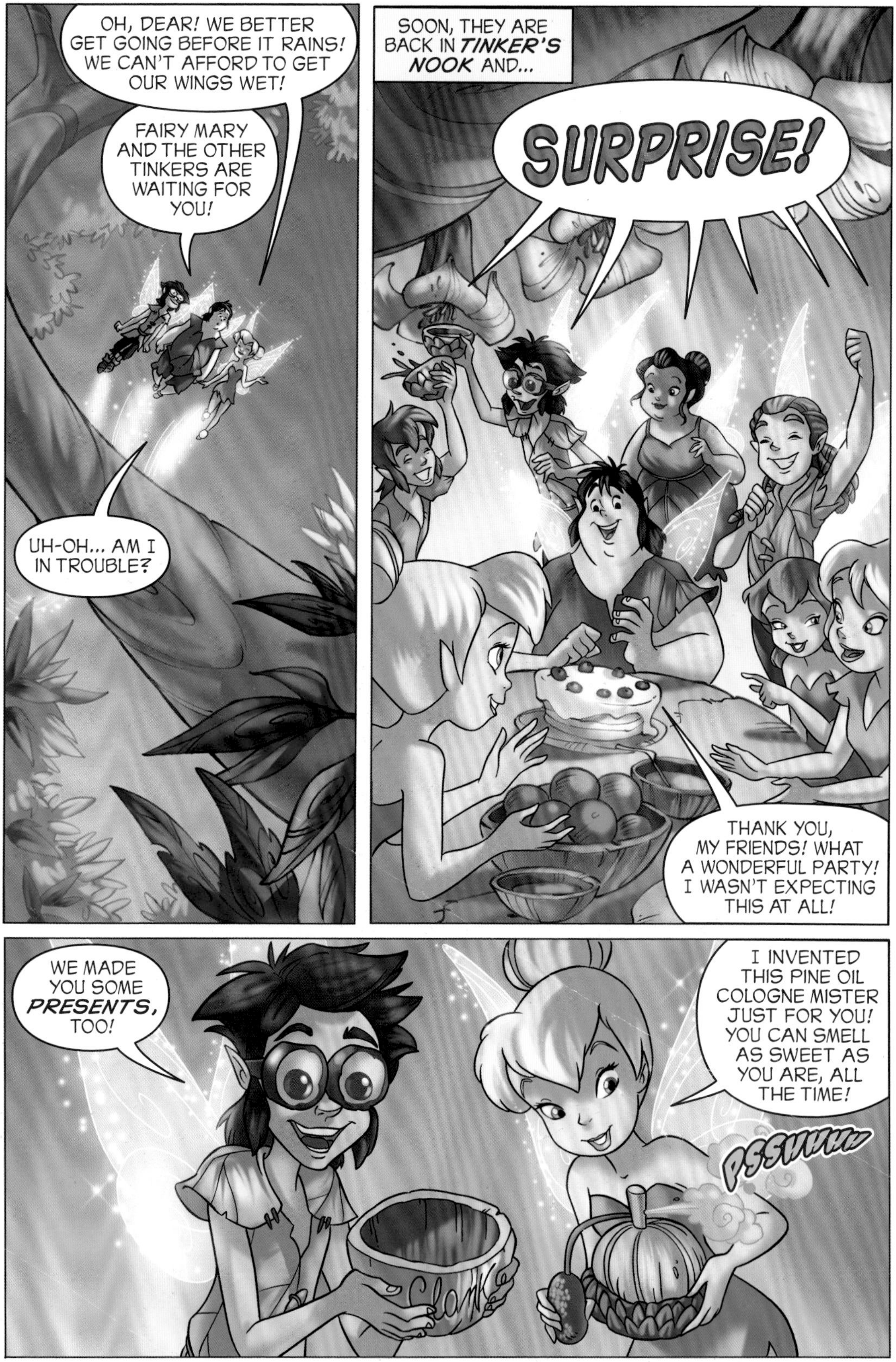
OH, DEAR! WE BETTER GET GOING BEFORE IT RAINS! WE CAN'T AFFORD TO GET OUR WINGS WET!
FAIRY MARY AND THE OTHER TINKERS ARE WAITING FOR YOU!
UH-OH... AM I IN TROUBLE?
SOON, THEY ARE BACK IN TINKER'S NOOK AND...
SURPRISE!
THANK YOU, MY FRIENDS! WHAT A WONDERFUL PARTY! I WASN'T EXPECTING THIS AT ALL!
WE MADE YOU SOME PRESENTS, TOO!
I INVENTED THIS PINE OIL COLOGNE MISTER JUST FOR YOU! YOU CAN SMELL AS SWEET AS YOU ARE, ALL THE TIME!
PSSWWW

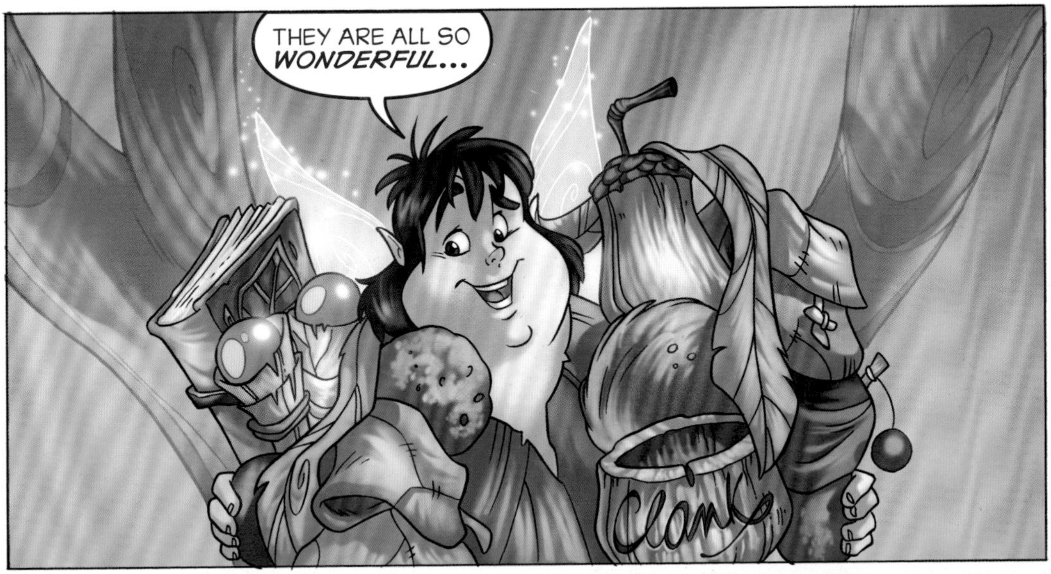
THEY ARE ALL SO WONDERFUL...
Clank

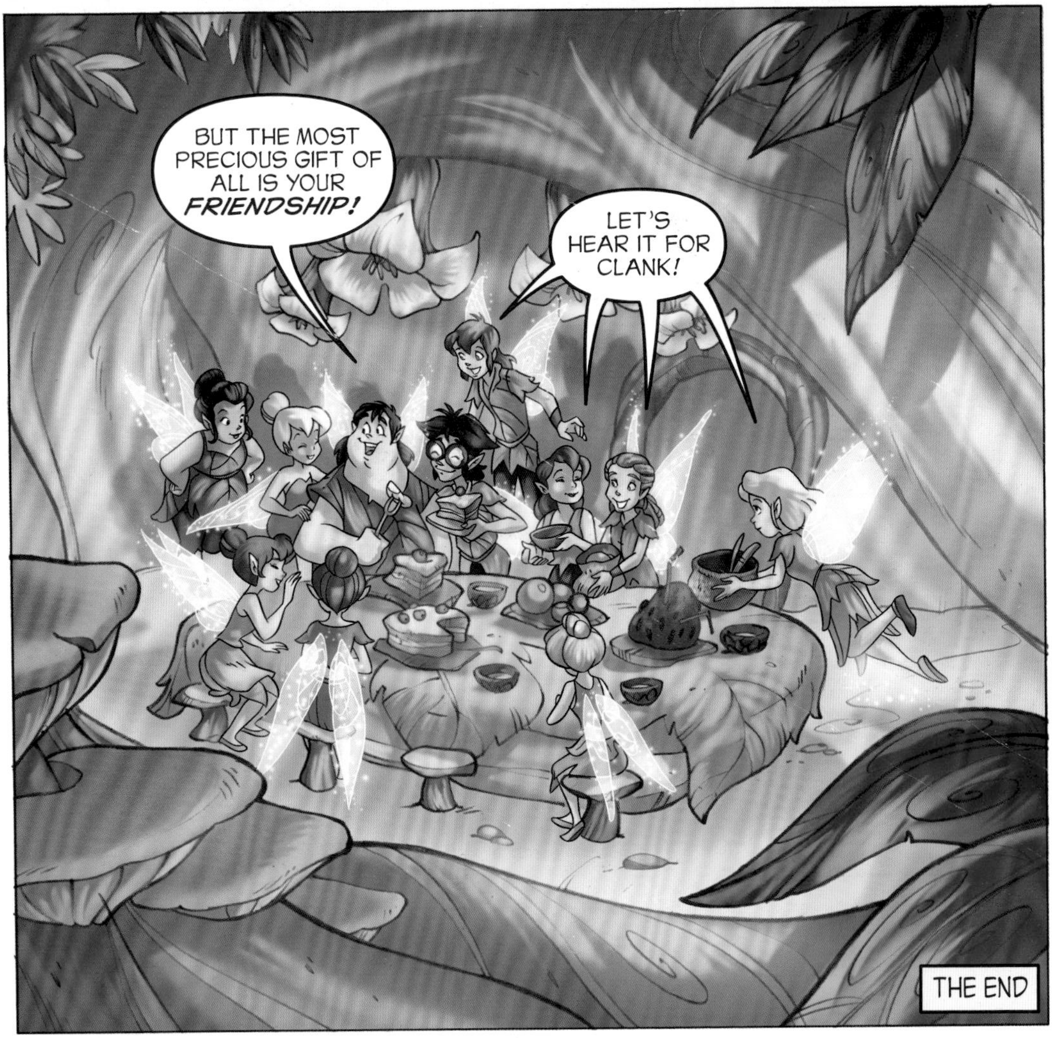
BUT THE MOST PRECIOUS GIFT OF ALL IS YOUR FRIENDSHIP!
LET'S HEAR IT FOR CLANK!
THE END

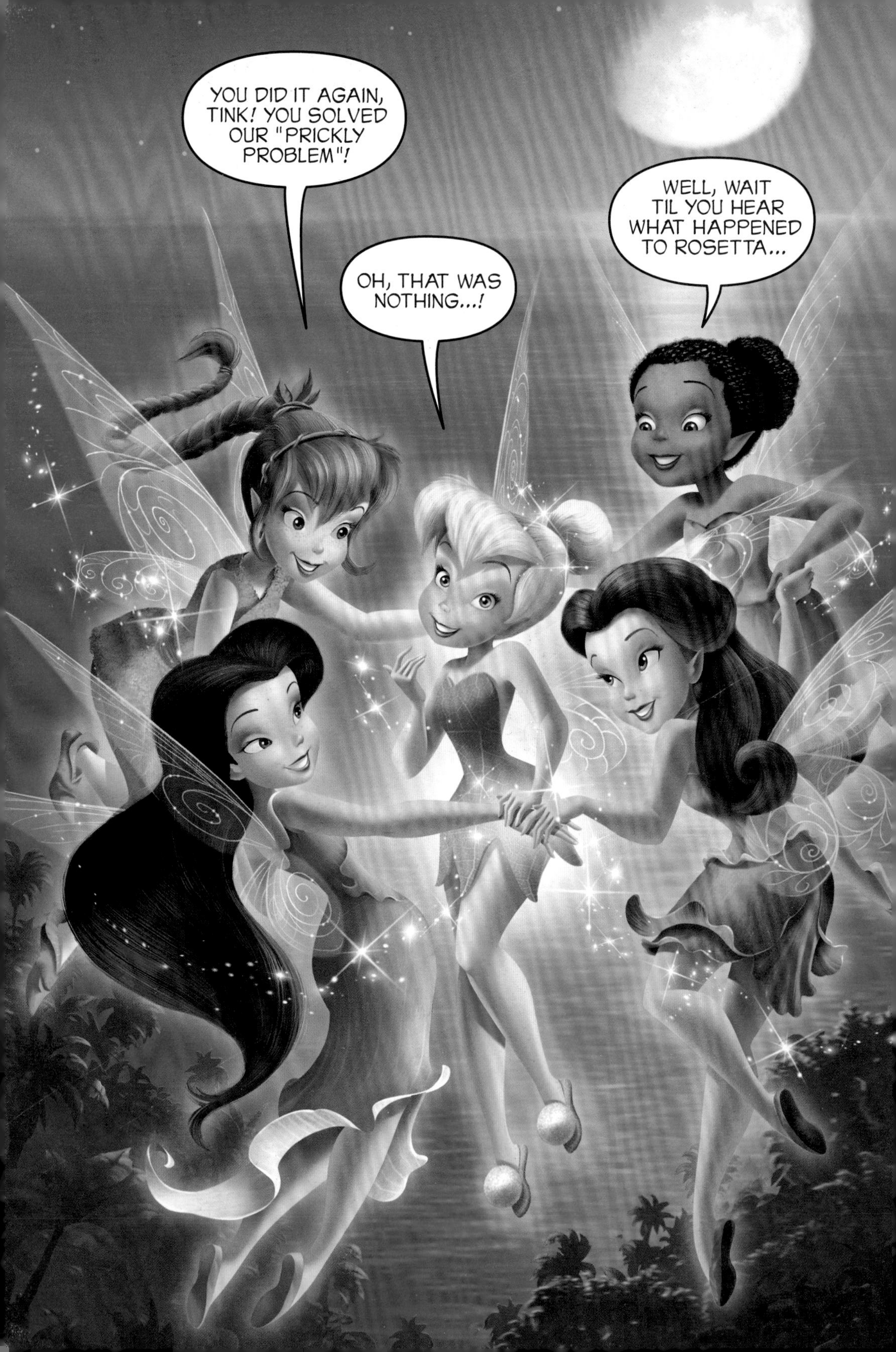
YOU DID IT AGAIN, TINK! YOU SOLVED OUR "PRICKLY PROBLEM"!
OH, THAT WAS NOTHING...!
WELL, WAIT TIL YOU HEAR WHAT HAPPENED TO ROSETTA...

A PRICKLY PROBLEM

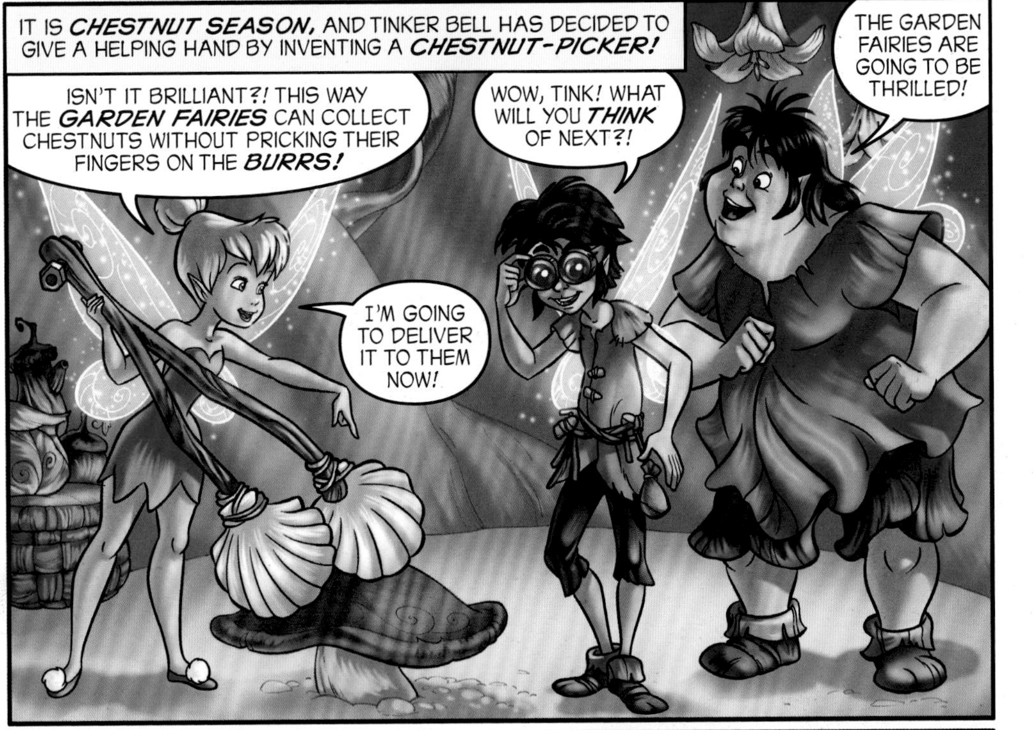

IT IS CHESTNUT SEASON, AND TINKER BELL HAS DECIDED TO GIVE A HELPING HAND BY INVENTING A CHESTNUT-PICKER!
ISN'T IT BRILLIANT?! THIS WAY THE GARDEN FAIRIES CAN COLLECT CHESTNUTS WITHOUT PRICKING THEIR FINGERS ON THE BURRS!
WOW, TINK! WHAT WILL YOU THINK OF NEXT?!
THE GARDEN FAIRIES ARE GOING TO BE THRILLED!
I'M GOING TO DELIVER IT TO THEM NOW!

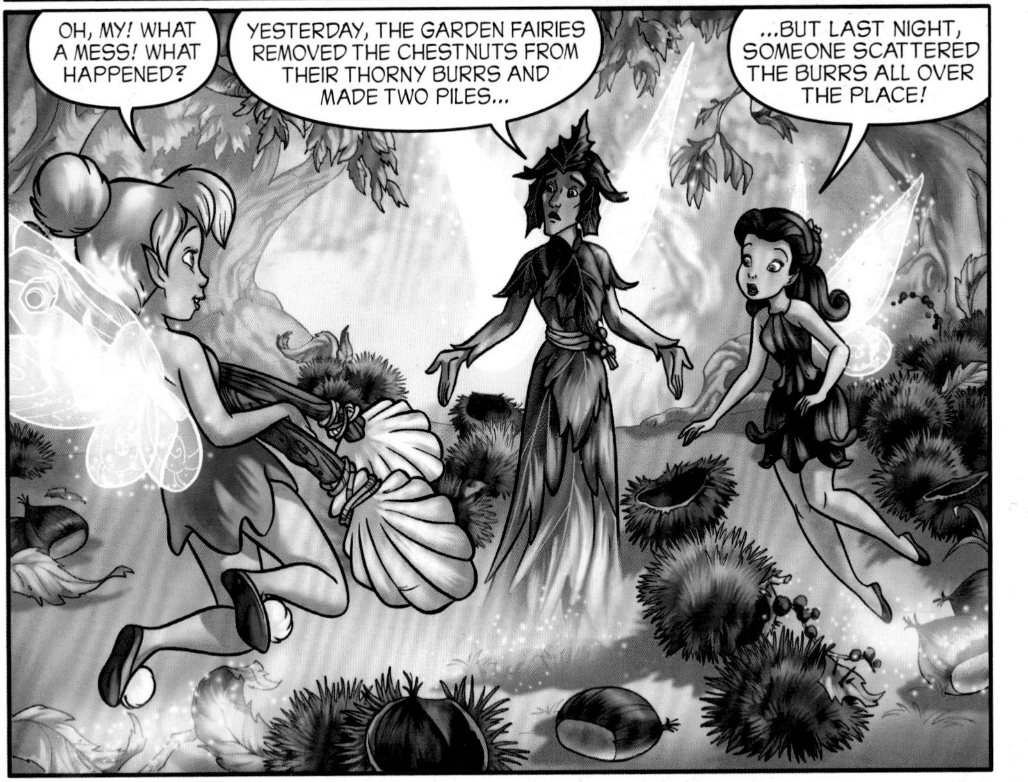

OH, MY! WHAT A MESS! WHAT HAPPENED?
YESTERDAY, THE GARDEN FAIRIES REMOVED THE CHESTNUTS FROM THEIR THORNY BURRS AND MADE TWO PILES...
...BUT LAST NIGHT, SOMEONE SCATTERED THE BURRS ALL OVER THE PLACE!

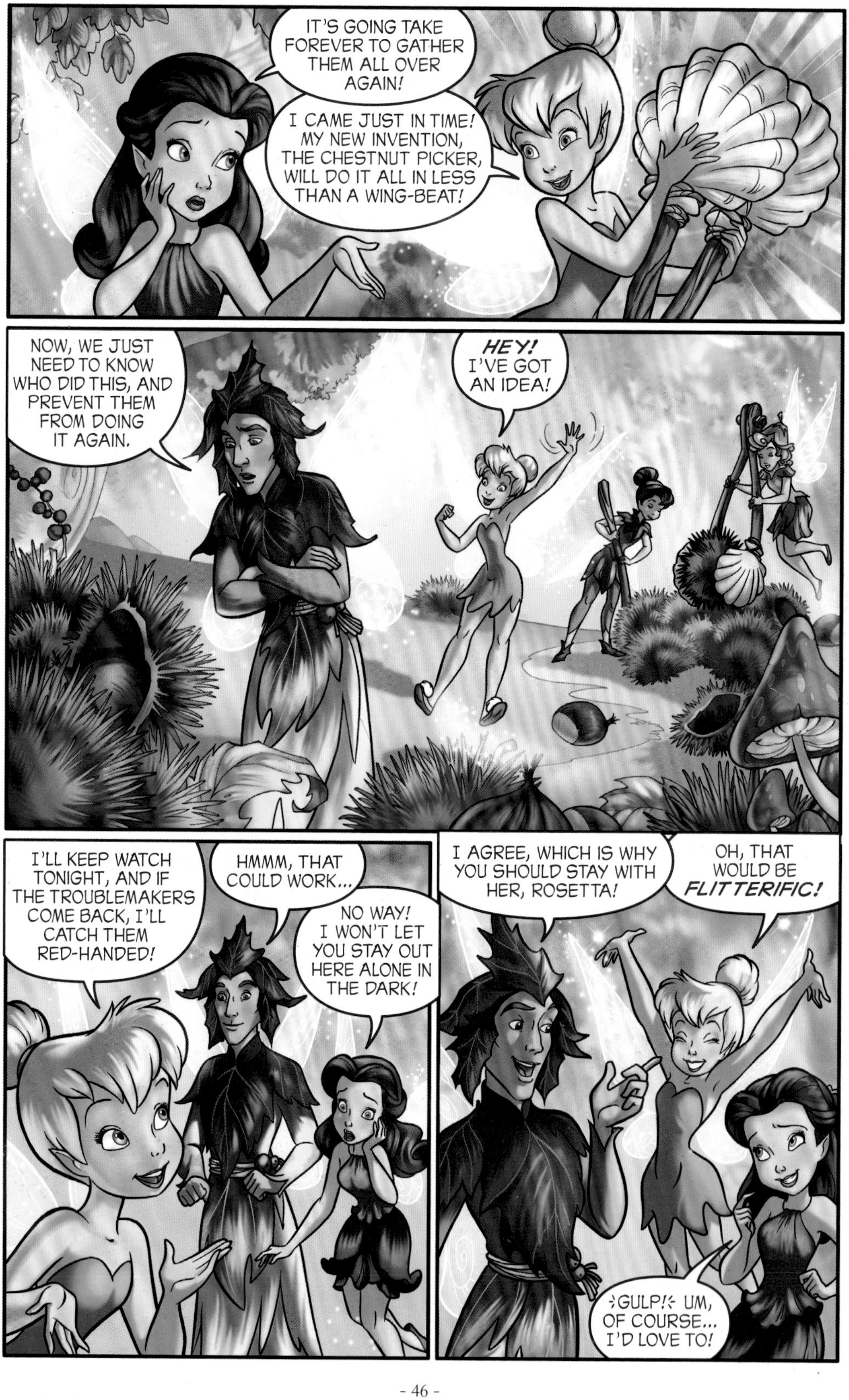
IT'S GOING TAKE FOREVER TO GATHER THEM ALL OVER AGAIN!
I CAME JUST IN TIME! MY NEW INVENTION, THE CHESTNUT PICKER, WILL DO IT ALL IN LESS THAN A WING-BEAT!
NOW, WE JUST NEED TO KNOW WHO DID THIS, AND PREVENT THEM FROM DOING IT AGAIN.
HEY! I'VE GOT AN IDEA!
I'LL KEEP WATCH TONIGHT, AND IF THE TROUBLEMAKERS COME BACK, I'LL CATCH THEM RED-HANDED!
HMMM, THAT COULD WORK...
NO WAY! I WON'T LET YOU STAY OUT HERE ALONE IN THE DARK!
I AGREE, WHICH IS WHY YOU SHOULD STAY WITH HER, ROSETTA!
OH, THAT WOULD BE FLITTERIFIC!
GULP! UM, OF COURSE... I'D LOVE TO!

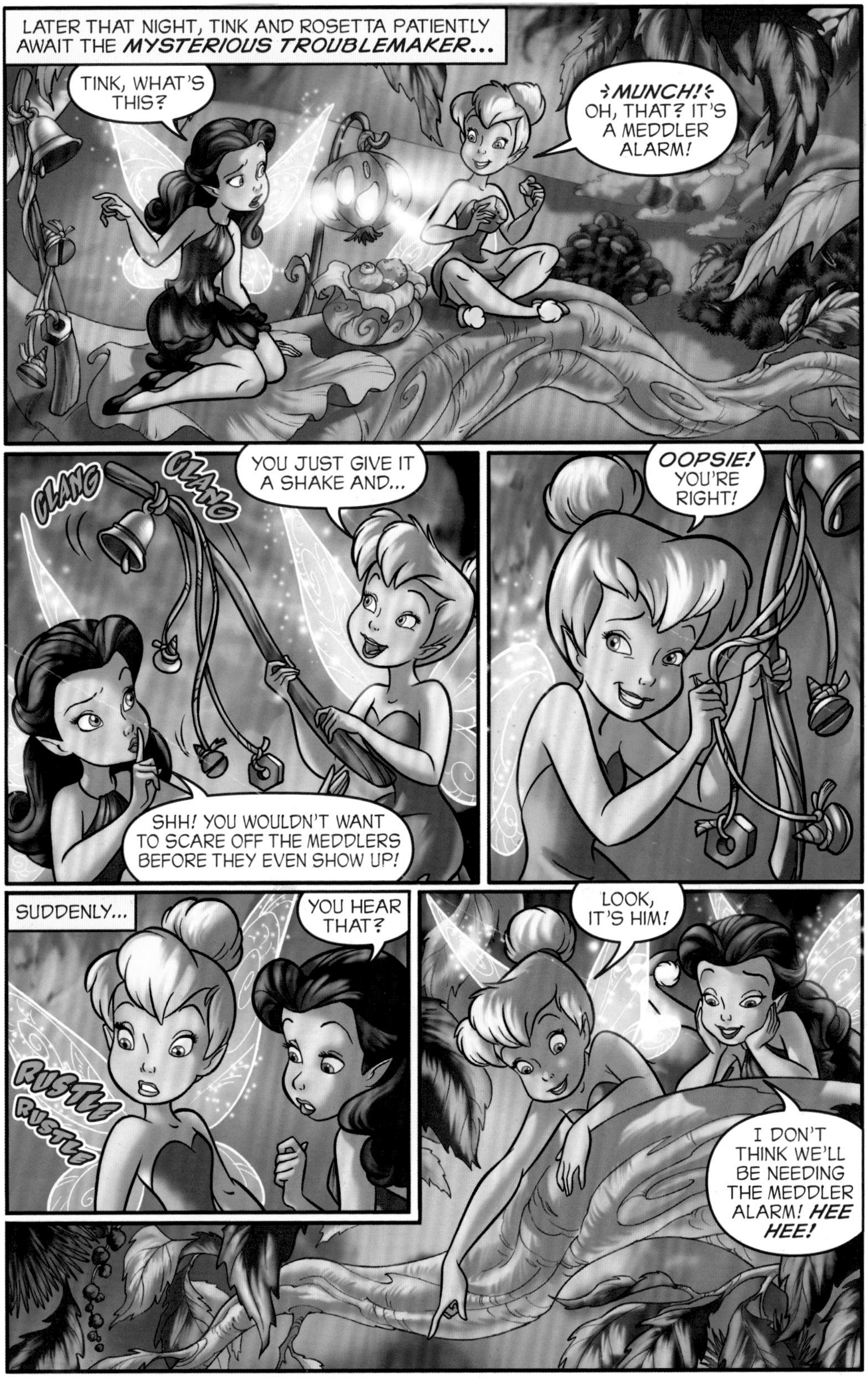
LATER THAT NIGHT, TINK AND ROSETTA PATIENTLY AWAIT THE MYSTERIOUS TROUBLEMAKER...
TINK, WHAT'S THIS?
MUNCH! OH, THAT? IT'S A MEDDLER ALARM!
YOU JUST GIVE IT A SHAKE AND...
CLANG
CLANG
SHH! YOU WOULDN'T WANT TO SCARE OFF THE MEDDLERS BEFORE THEY EVEN SHOW UP!
OOPSIE! YOU'RE RIGHT!
SUDDENLY...
YOU HEAR THAT?
RUSTLE
RUSTLE
LOOK, IT'S HIM!
I DON'T THINK WE'LL BE NEEDING THE MEDDLER ALARM! HEE HEE!

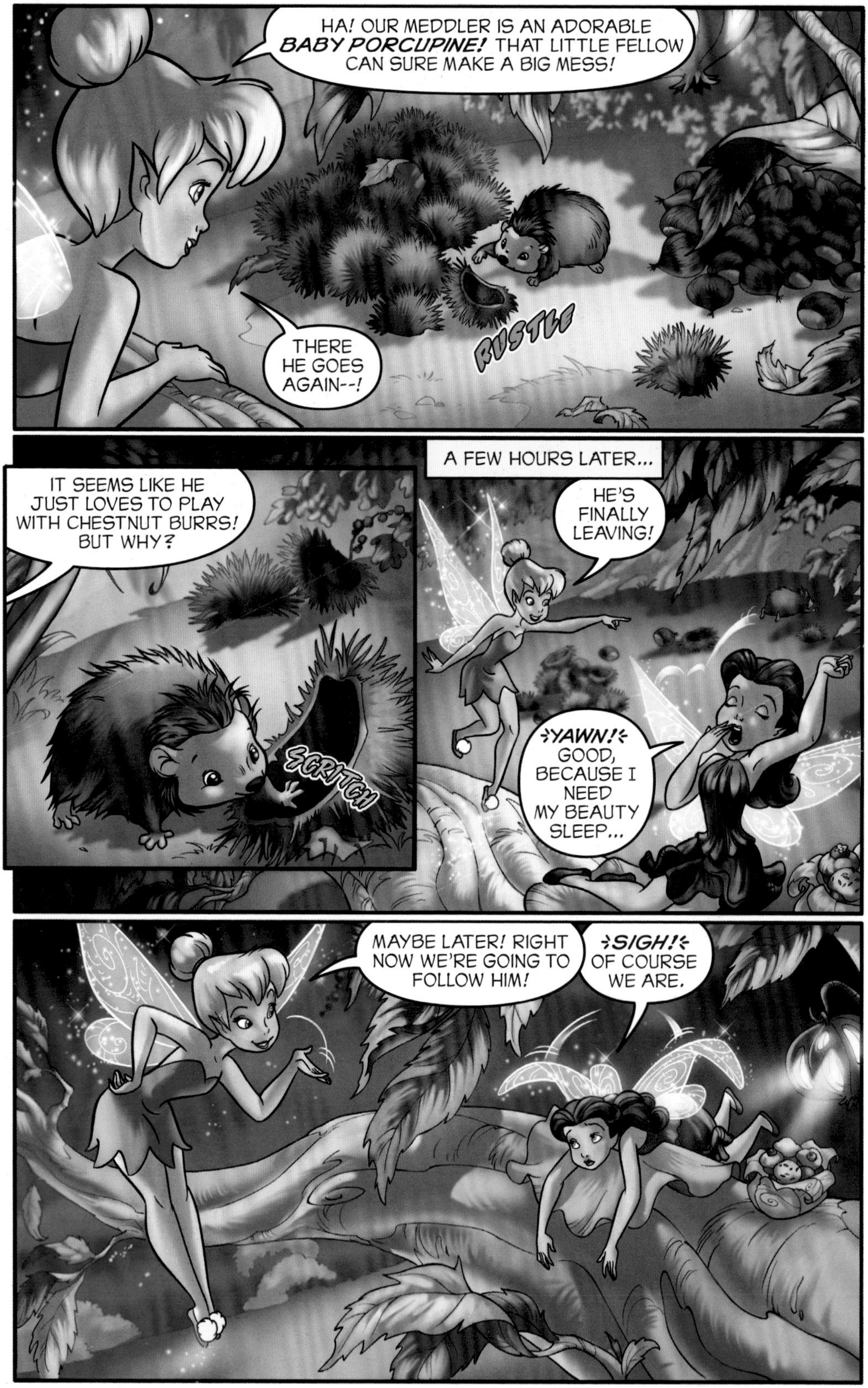

HA! OUR MEDDLER IS AN ADORABLE BABY PORCUPINE! THAT LITTLE FELLOW CAN SURE MAKE A BIG MESS!
THERE HE GOES AGAIN--!
RUSTLE
IT SEEMS LIKE HE JUST LOVES TO PLAY WITH CHESTNUT BURRS! BUT WHY?
SCRITCH
A FEW HOURS LATER...
HE'S FINALLY LEAVING!
YAWN! GOOD, BECAUSE I NEED MY BEAUTY SLEEP...
MAYBE LATER! RIGHT NOW WE'RE GOING TO FOLLOW HIM!
SIGH! OF COURSE WE ARE.

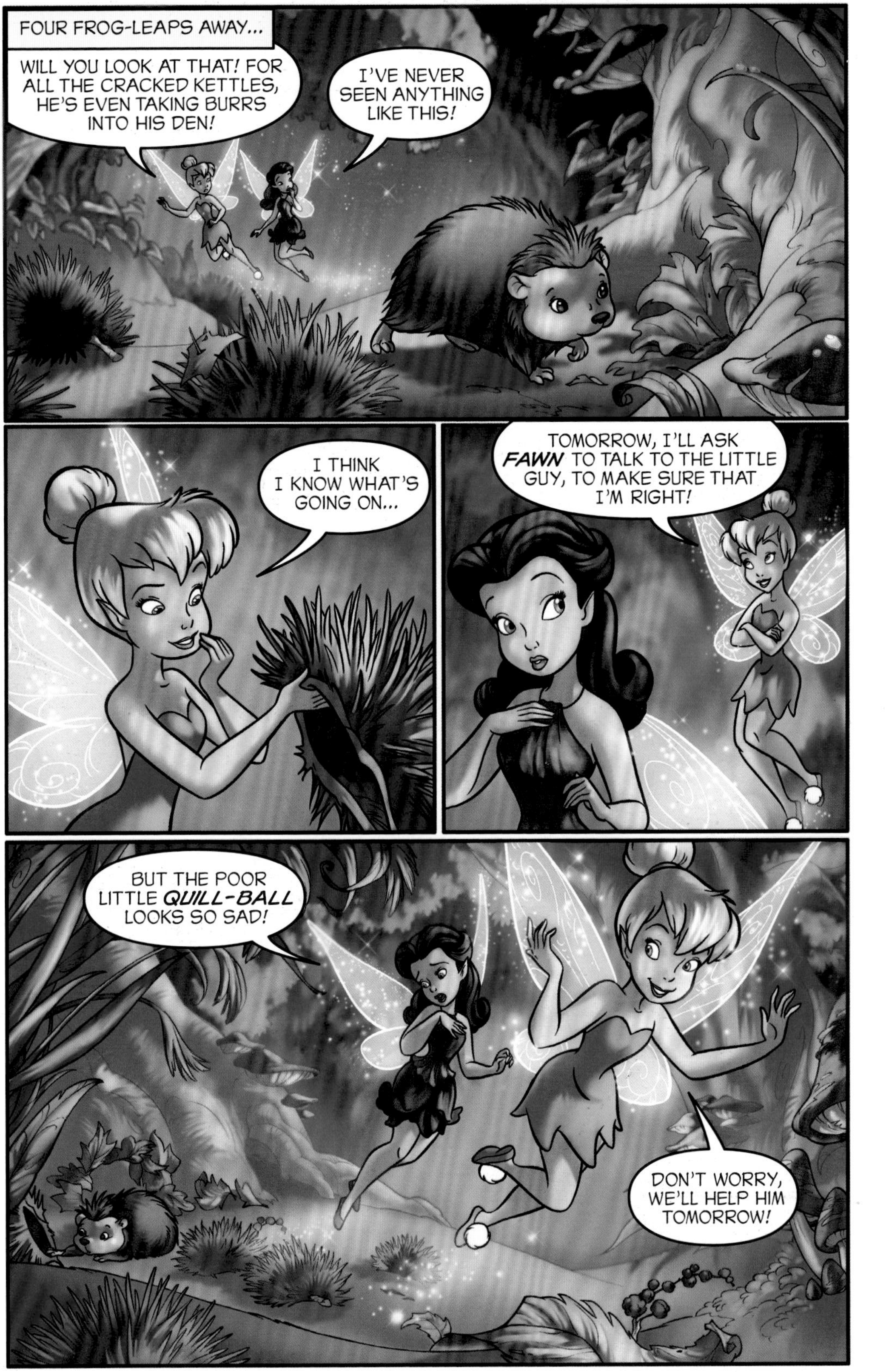
FOUR FROG-LEAPS AWAY...
WILL YOU LOOK AT THAT! FOR ALL THE CRACKED KETTLES, HE'S EVEN TAKING BURRS INTO HIS DEN!
I'VE NEVER SEEN ANYTHING LIKE THIS!
I THINK I KNOW WHAT'S GOING ON...
TOMORROW, I'LL ASK FAWN TO TALK TO THE LITTLE GUY, TO MAKE SURE THAT I'M RIGHT!
BUT THE POOR LITTLE QUILL-BALL LOOKS SO SAD!
DON'T WORRY, WE'LL HELP HIM TOMORROW!

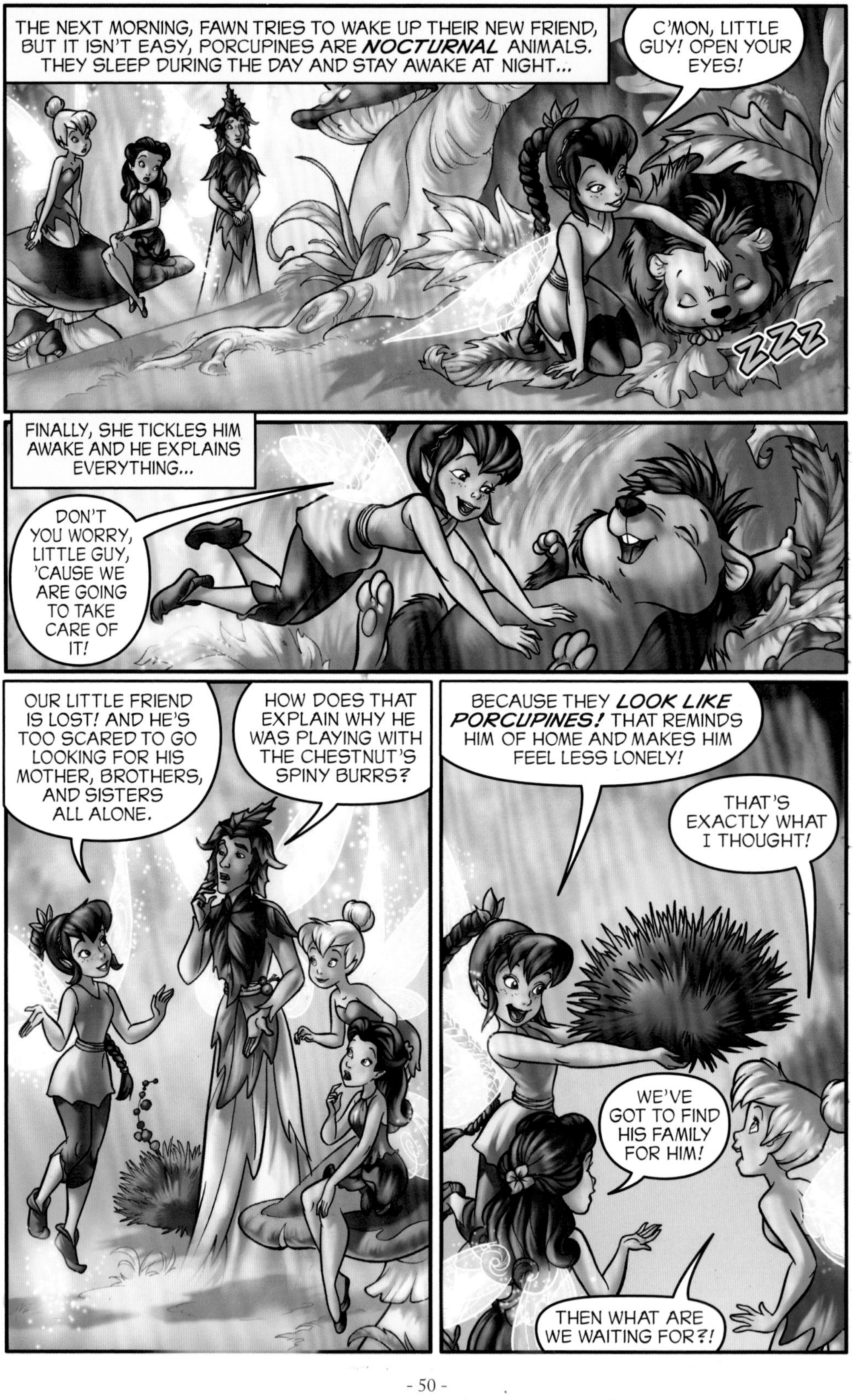
THE NEXT MORNING, FAWN TRIES TO WAKE UP THEIR NEW FRIEND, BUT IT ISN'T EASY, PORCUPINES ARE ***NOCTURNAL*** ANIMALS. THEY SLEEP DURING THE DAY AND STAY AWAKE AT NIGHT...
C'MON, LITTLE GUY! OPEN YOUR EYES!
ZZZ
FINALLY, SHE TICKLES HIM AWAKE AND HE EXPLAINS EVERYTHING...
DON'T YOU WORRY, LITTLE GUY, 'CAUSE WE ARE GOING TO TAKE CARE OF IT!
OUR LITTLE FRIEND IS LOST! AND HE'S TOO SCARED TO GO LOOKING FOR HIS MOTHER, BROTHERS, AND SISTERS ALL ALONE.
HOW DOES THAT EXPLAIN WHY HE WAS PLAYING WITH THE CHESTNUT'S SPINY BURRS?
BECAUSE THEY ***LOOK LIKE PORCUPINES!*** THAT REMINDS HIM OF HOME AND MAKES HIM FEEL LESS LONELY!
THAT'S EXACTLY WHAT I THOUGHT!
WE'VE GOT TO FIND HIS FAMILY FOR HIM!
THEN WHAT ARE WE WAITING FOR?!

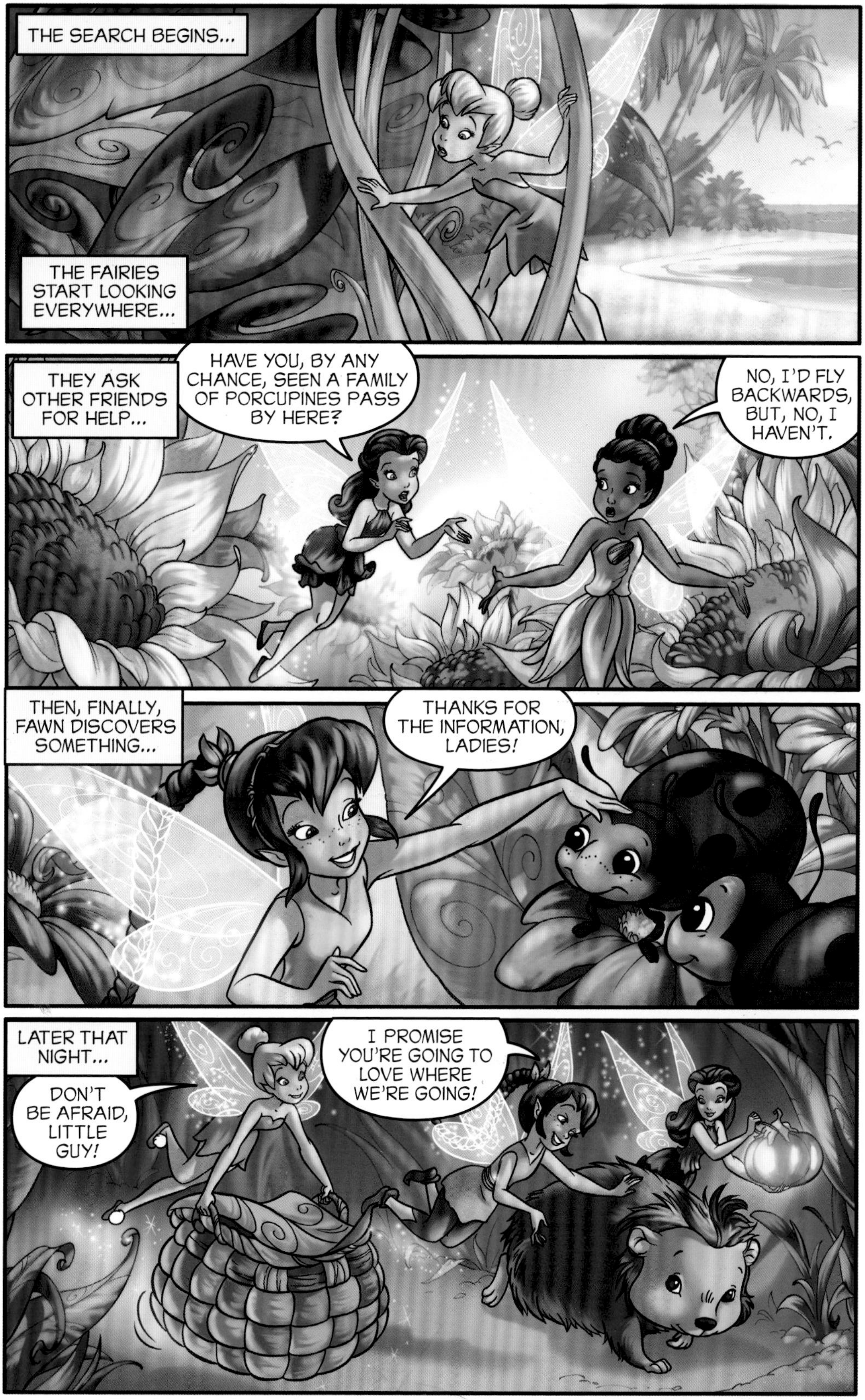
THE SEARCH BEGINS...
THE FAIRIES START LOOKING EVERYWHERE...
THEY ASK OTHER FRIENDS FOR HELP...
HAVE YOU, BY ANY CHANCE, SEEN A FAMILY OF PORCUPINES PASS BY HERE?
NO, I'D FLY BACKWARDS, BUT, NO, I HAVEN'T.
THEN, FINALLY, FAWN DISCOVERS SOMETHING...
THANKS FOR THE INFORMATION, LADIES!
LATER THAT NIGHT...
DON'T BE AFRAID, LITTLE GUY!
I PROMISE YOU'RE GOING TO LOVE WHERE WE'RE GOING!

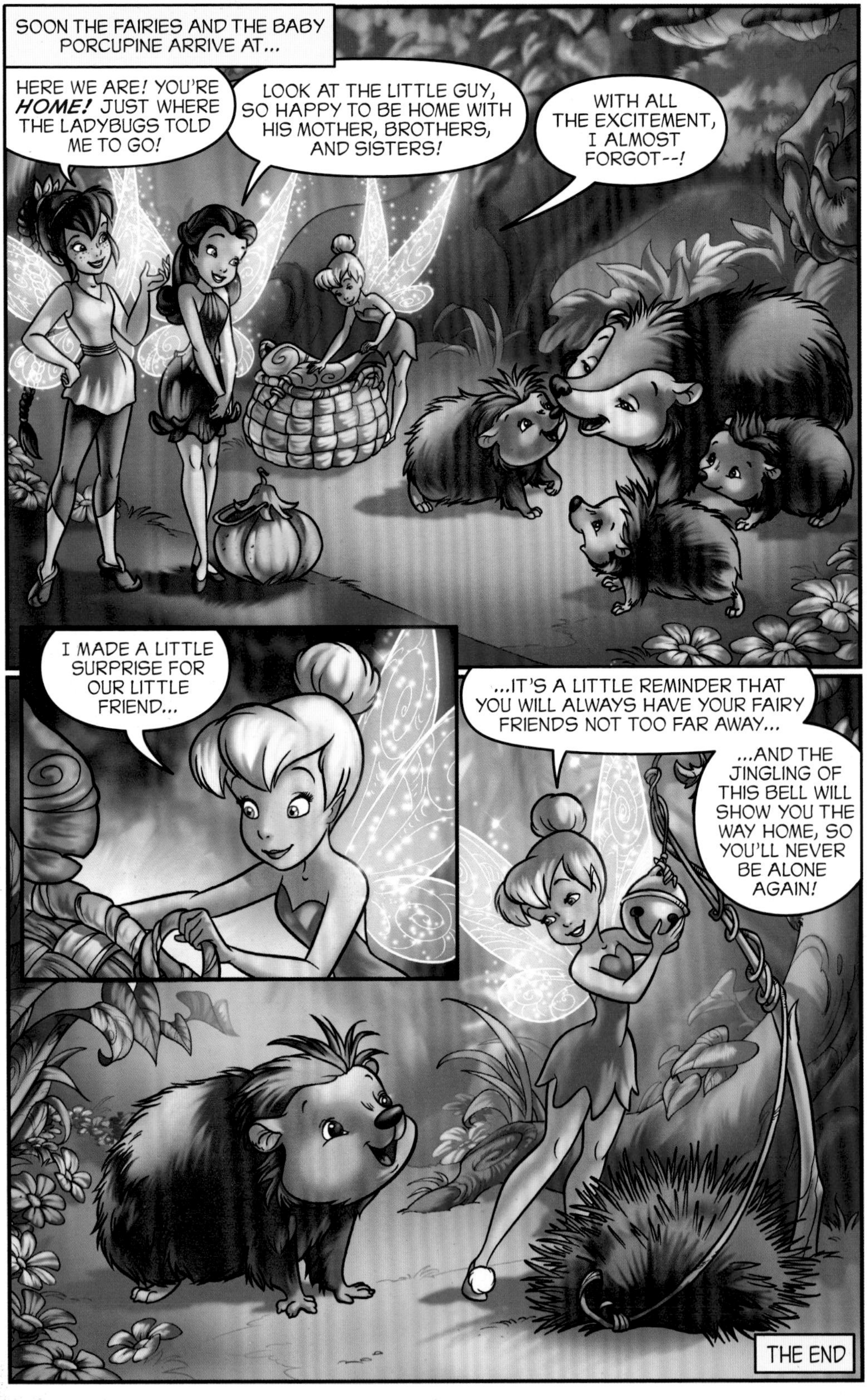
SOON THE FAIRIES AND THE BABY PORCUPINE ARRIVE AT...
HERE WE ARE! YOU'RE **HOME!** JUST WHERE THE LADYBUGS TOLD ME TO GO!
LOOK AT THE LITTLE GUY, SO HAPPY TO BE HOME WITH HIS MOTHER, BROTHERS, AND SISTERS!
WITH ALL THE EXCITEMENT, I ALMOST FORGOT--!
I MADE A LITTLE SURPRISE FOR OUR LITTLE FRIEND...
...IT'S A LITTLE REMINDER THAT YOU WILL ALWAYS HAVE YOUR FAIRY FRIENDS NOT TOO FAR AWAY...
...AND THE JINGLING OF THIS BELL WILL SHOW YOU THE WAY HOME, SO YOU'LL NEVER BE ALONE AGAIN!
THE END

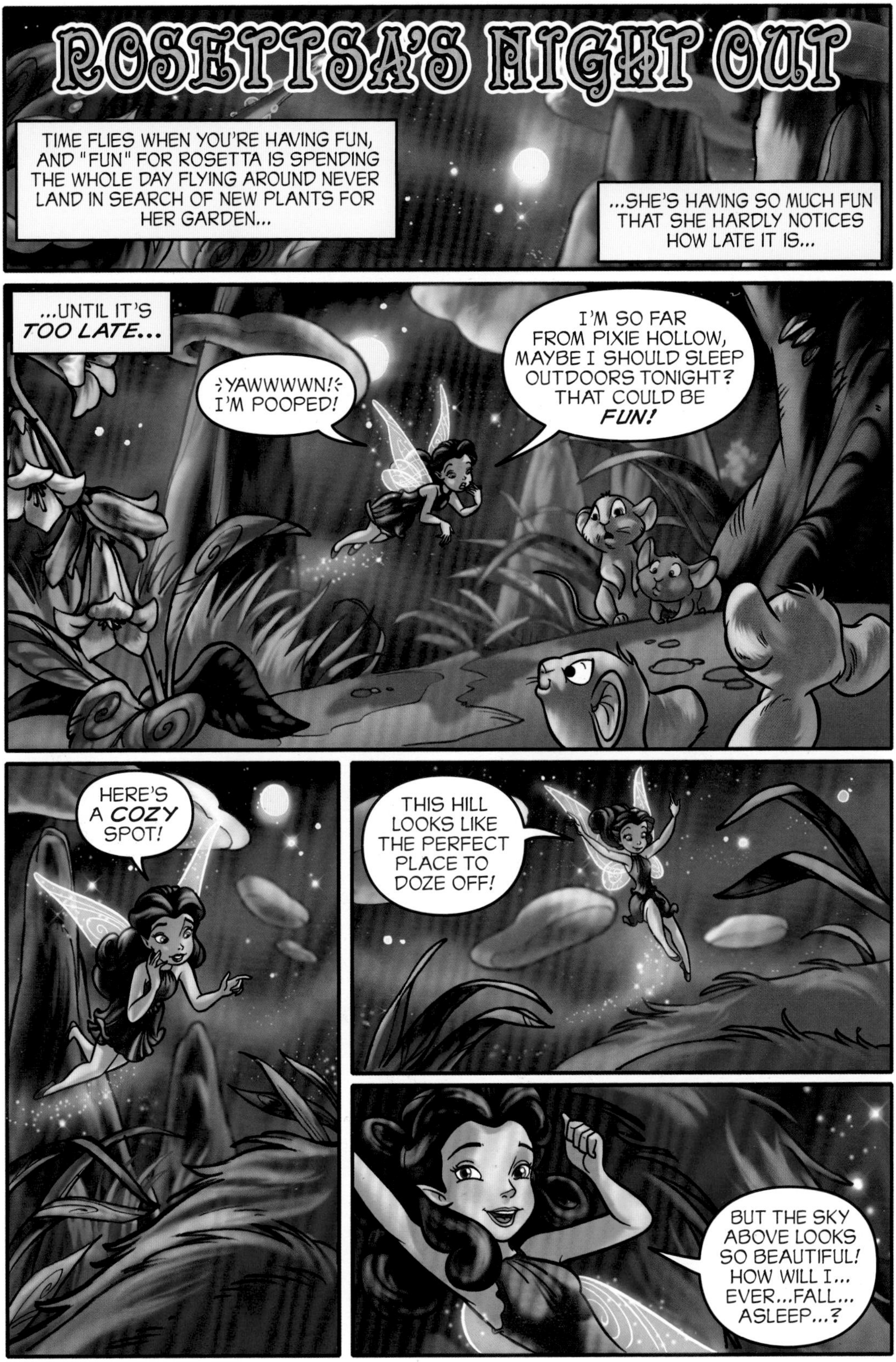
ROSETTSA'S NIGHT OUT
TIME FLIES WHEN YOU'RE HAVING FUN, AND "FUN" FOR ROSETTA IS SPENDING THE WHOLE DAY FLYING AROUND NEVER LAND IN SEARCH OF NEW PLANTS FOR HER GARDEN...
...SHE'S HAVING SO MUCH FUN THAT SHE HARDLY NOTICES HOW LATE IT IS...
...UNTIL IT'S *TOO LATE...*
YAWWWWN! I'M POOPED!
I'M SO FAR FROM PIXIE HOLLOW, MAYBE I SHOULD SLEEP OUTDOORS TONIGHT? THAT COULD BE *FUN!*
HERE'S A *COZY* SPOT!
THIS HILL LOOKS LIKE THE PERFECT PLACE TO DOZE OFF!
BUT THE SKY ABOVE LOOKS SO BEAUTIFUL! HOW WILL I... EVER...FALL... ASLEEP...?

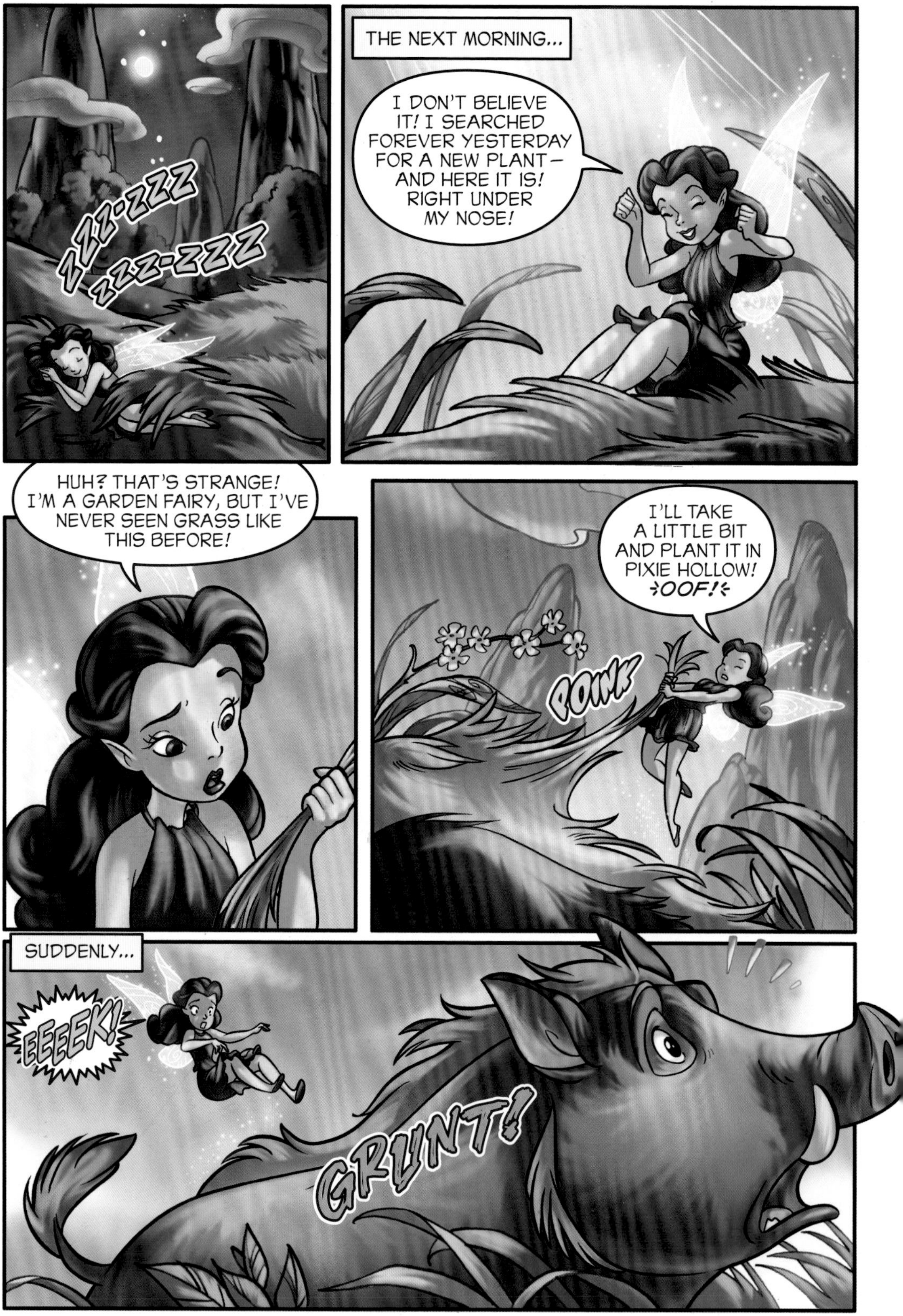
ZZZ-ZZZ
ZZZ-ZZZ
THE NEXT MORNING...
I DON'T BELIEVE IT! I SEARCHED FOREVER YESTERDAY FOR A NEW PLANT— AND HERE IT IS! RIGHT UNDER MY NOSE!
HUH? THAT'S STRANGE! I'M A GARDEN FAIRY, BUT I'VE NEVER SEEN GRASS LIKE THIS BEFORE!
I'LL TAKE A LITTLE BIT AND PLANT IT IN PIXIE HOLLOW! OOF!
POINK
SUDDENLY...
EEEEK!
GRUNT!

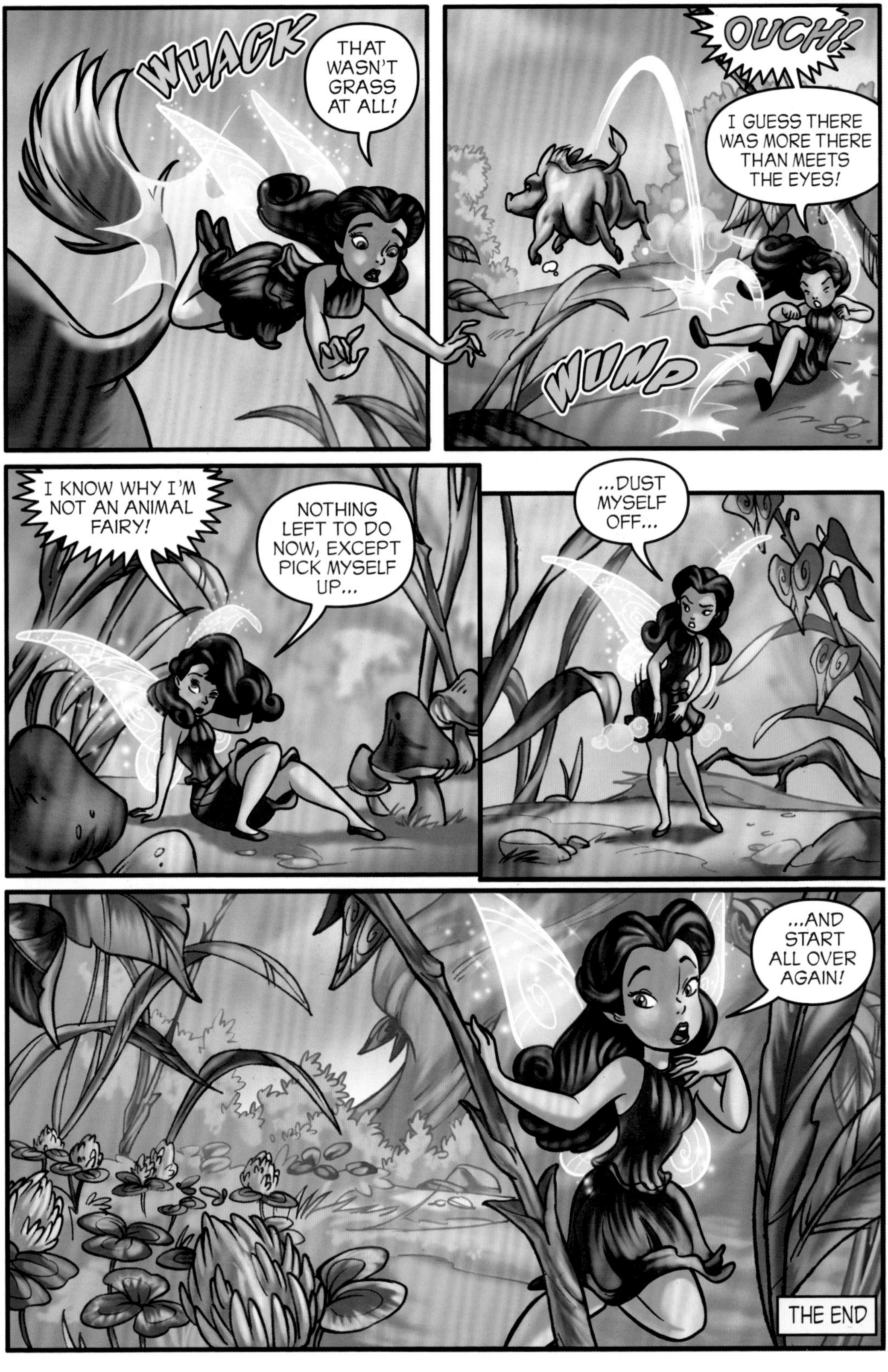
WHACK
THAT WASN'T GRASS AT ALL!
OUCH!
I GUESS THERE WAS MORE THERE THAN MEETS THE EYES!
WUMP
I KNOW WHY I'M NOT AN ANIMAL FAIRY!
NOTHING LEFT TO DO NOW, EXCEPT PICK MYSELF UP...
...DUST MYSELF OFF...
...AND START ALL OVER AGAIN!
THE END

Presenting an all-new series from

PAPERCUTZ™

Nancy Drew
and The Clue Crew
#1
SMALL VOLCANOES
Sarah Kinney
Stefan Petrucha
Stan Goldberg
Based on the

Nancy Drew
and The Clue Crew
#2
SECRET SAND SLEUTHS
PAPERCUTZ
Sarah Kinney
Stan Goldberg
Based on the series by
Carolyn Keene

Available Now!

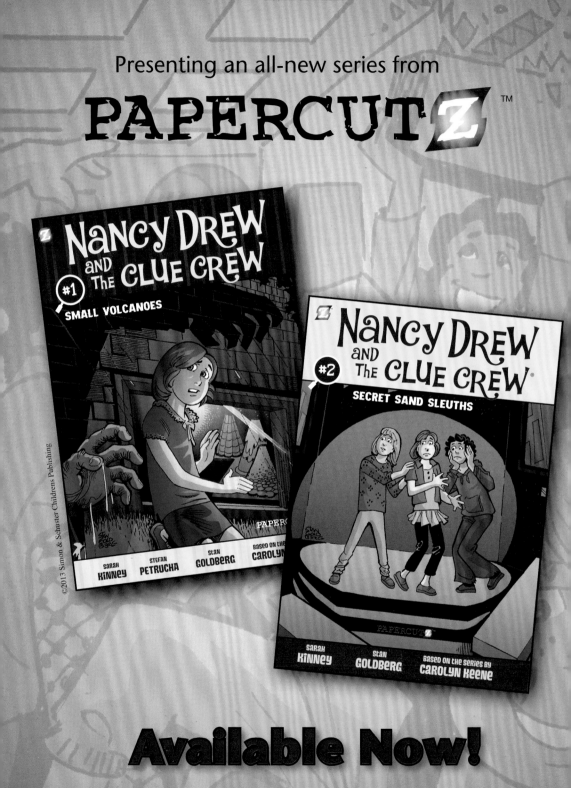

WATCH OUT FOR PAPERCUTZ

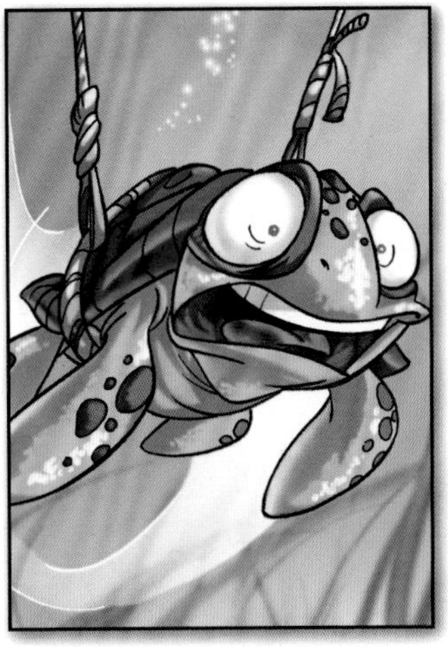

Welcome to the eleventh, enchanted DISNEY FAIRIES graphic novel from Papercutz, those Lost Boys and Girls dedicated to publishing great graphic novels for all ages! I'm Jim Salicrup, the Editor-in-Chief and part-time Pixie Hollow Tour Guide.

In "Where There's a Dream, There's a Way," we meet a young turtle who has a dream—she wants to fly like a fairy! I bet she just saw "Dumbo" on DVD and thought "if an elephant can fly, why, oh, why can't I?" (She might've just seen "The Wizard of Oz" too.) She was super lucky to run into Tinker Bell—if anyone can help make your dreams come true, Tink sure can!

In DISNEY FAIRIES #10, I wrote that "when I was just a child, one of my dreams was to work in comics." And like that turtle, I was super-lucky too! My dream came true when I was just fifteen, and I've been working away in comics ever since. So, I really do believe that dreams can come true, but I also know it isn't always that easy. Sometimes, you can try and try and try, and it seems like your dream is never going to come true. But if that turtle could fly, and I can work in comics, maybe your dream can come true too!

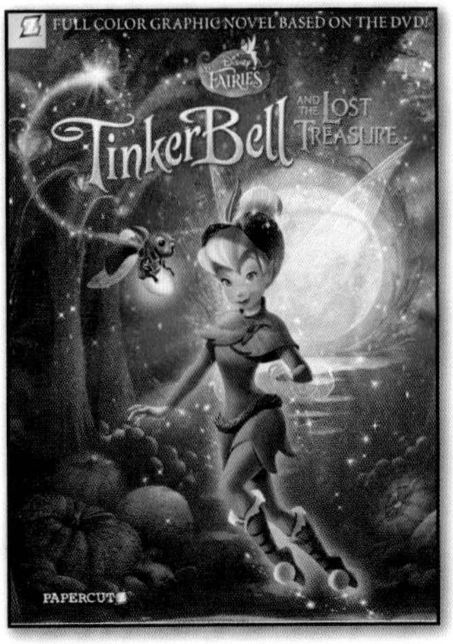
FULL COLOR GRAPHIC NOVEL BASED ON THE DVD!
FAIRIES
TinkerBell AND THE LOST TREASURE
PAPERCUTZ

One of the countless reasons I dreamed of working in comics was to meet such amazing cartoonists as Stan Goldberg. While I haven't actually met in-person such great DISNEY FAIRIES artists as Antonello Dalena, Manuela Razzi, or Sara Storino yet, I have met Mr. Goldberg. As a kid I loved his work on MILLIE THE MODEL and CHILI from Marvel Comics, and for years he's been the top artist over at Archie Comics. Recently Stan received the National Cartoonists Society's prestigious The Gold Key award, and entered the NCS Hall of Fame. And believe it or not he's even drawing an all-new series of graphic novels for Papercutz—NANCY DREW AND THE CLUE CREW. You can even see a preview on the following pages. Having Stan Goldberg at Papercutz is not only a great honor, it's yet another dream come true!

Hey, want to help make another dream come true? Then don't miss DISNEY FAIRIES #12 "Tinker Bell and the Lost Treasure." After all, how can my dream of Papercutz becoming the most successful graphic novel publisher come true without you? And if you want your dreams to come true too, remember to keep believing in "faith, trust, and pixie dust"!

Thanks,

Jim

STAY IN TOUCH!

EMAIL:	salicrup@papercutz.com
WEB:	www.papercutz.com
TWITTER:	@papercutzgn
FACEBOOK:	PAPERCUTZGRAPHICNOVELS
REGULAR MAIL:	Papercutz, 160 Broadway, Suite 700, East Wing, New York, NY 10038

Special Preview of NANCY DREW AND THE CLUE CREW #2 "Secret Sand Sleuths"...

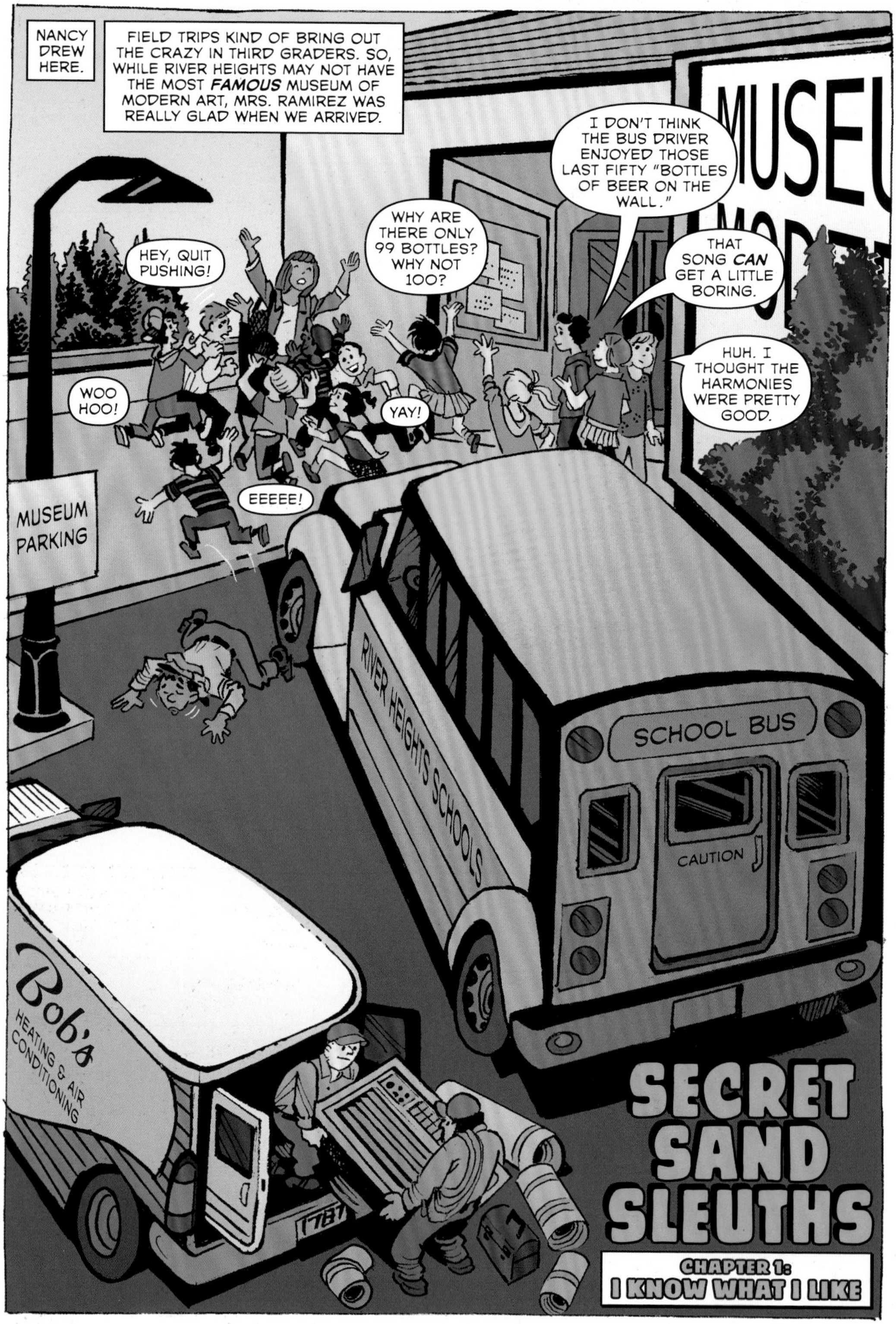
NANCY DREW HERE.
FIELD TRIPS KIND OF BRING OUT THE CRAZY IN THIRD GRADERS. SO, WHILE RIVER HEIGHTS MAY NOT HAVE THE MOST FAMOUS MUSEUM OF MODERN ART, MRS. RAMIREZ WAS REALLY GLAD WHEN WE ARRIVED.
MUSEU
I DON'T THINK THE BUS DRIVER ENJOYED THOSE LAST FIFTY "BOTTLES OF BEER ON THE WALL."
THAT SONG CAN GET A LITTLE BORING.
HUH. I THOUGHT THE HARMONIES WERE PRETTY GOOD.
WHY ARE THERE ONLY 99 BOTTLES? WHY NOT 100?
HEY, QUIT PUSHING!
WOO HOO!
YAY!
EEEEE!
MUSEUM PARKING
RIVER HEIGHTS SCHOOLS
SCHOOL BUS
CAUTION
Bob's HEATING & AIR CONDITIONING
SECRET SAND SLEUTHS
CHAPTER 1: I KNOW WHAT I LIKE

Sarah Kinney – Writer Stan Goldberg – Artist Laurie E. Smith – Colorist Tom Orzechowski – Letterer

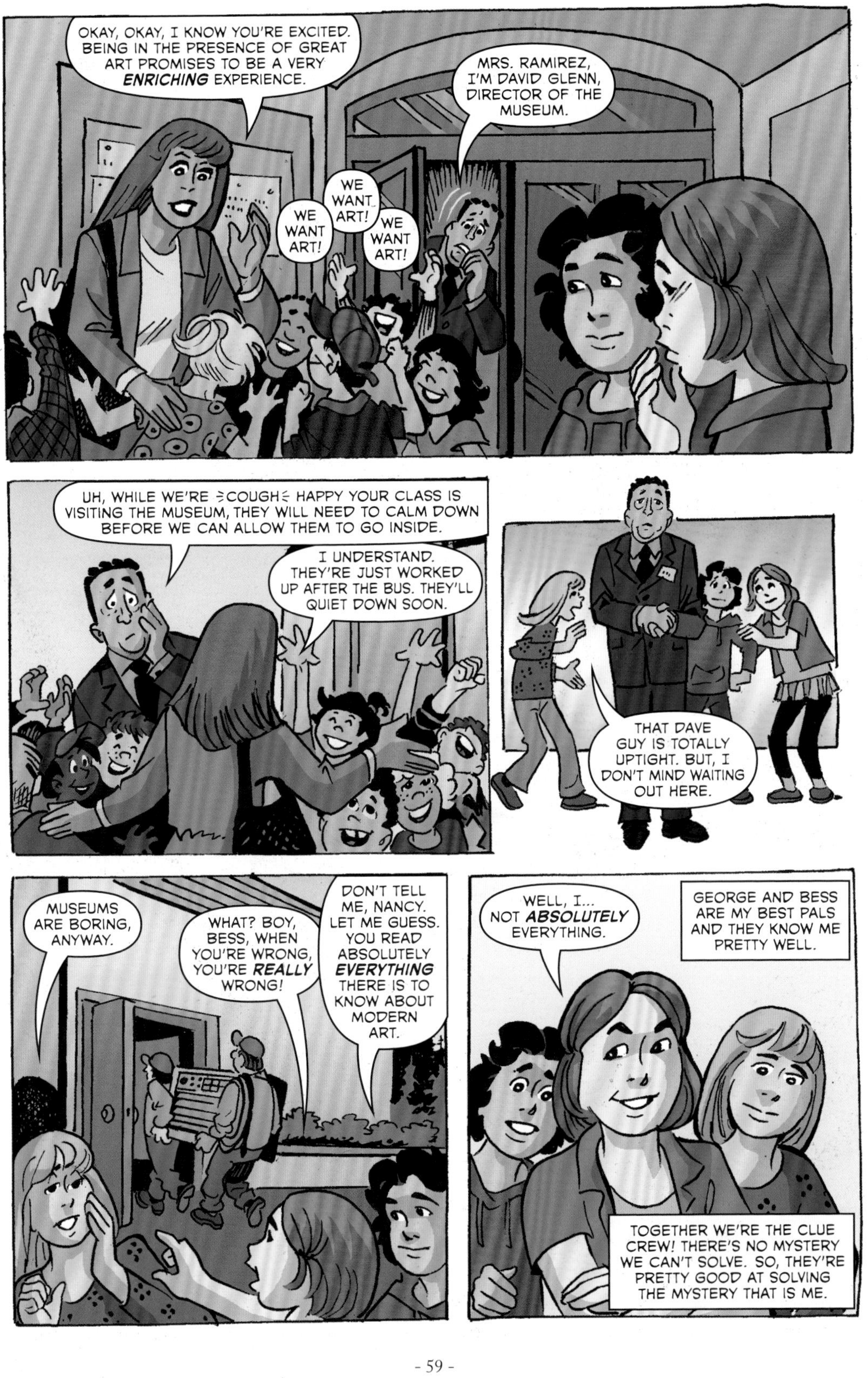
OKAY, OKAY, I KNOW YOU'RE EXCITED. BEING IN THE PRESENCE OF GREAT ART PROMISES TO BE A VERY ENRICHING EXPERIENCE.
WE WANT ART!
WE WANT ART!
WE WANT ART!
MRS. RAMIREZ, I'M DAVID GLENN, DIRECTOR OF THE MUSEUM.
UH, WHILE WE'RE ⋧COUGH⋦ HAPPY YOUR CLASS IS VISITING THE MUSEUM, THEY WILL NEED TO CALM DOWN BEFORE WE CAN ALLOW THEM TO GO INSIDE.
I UNDERSTAND. THEY'RE JUST WORKED UP AFTER THE BUS. THEY'LL QUIET DOWN SOON.
THAT DAVE GUY IS TOTALLY UPTIGHT. BUT, I DON'T MIND WAITING OUT HERE.
MUSEUMS ARE BORING, ANYWAY.
WHAT? BOY, BESS, WHEN YOU'RE WRONG, YOU'RE REALLY WRONG!
DON'T TELL ME, NANCY. LET ME GUESS. YOU READ ABSOLUTELY EVERYTHING THERE IS TO KNOW ABOUT MODERN ART.
WELL, I... NOT ABSOLUTELY EVERYTHING.
GEORGE AND BESS ARE MY BEST PALS AND THEY KNOW ME PRETTY WELL.
TOGETHER WE'RE THE CLUE CREW! THERE'S NO MYSTERY WE CAN'T SOLVE. SO, THEY'RE PRETTY GOOD AT SOLVING THE MYSTERY THAT IS ME.

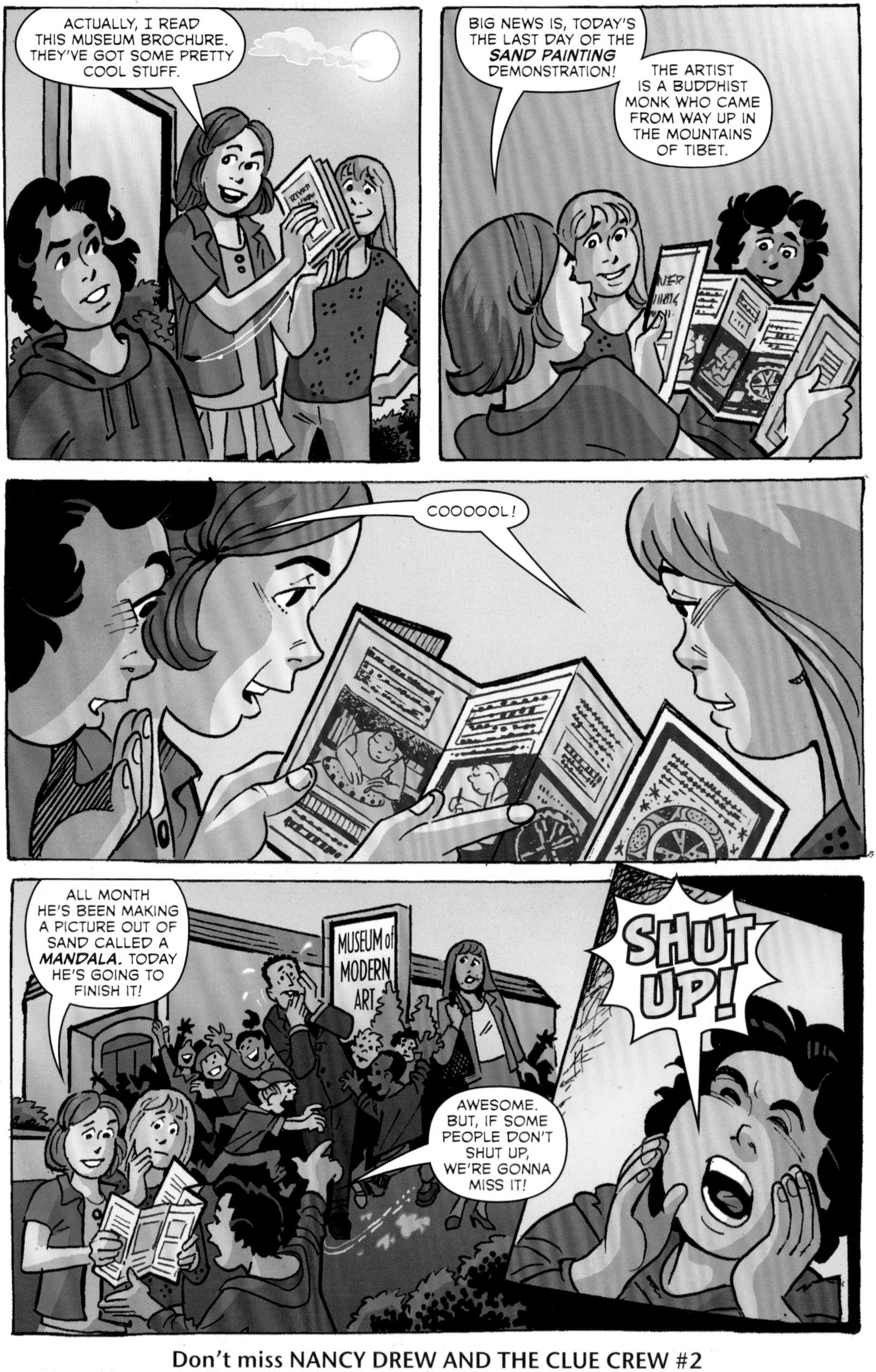
ACTUALLY, I READ THIS MUSEUM BROCHURE. THEY'VE GOT SOME PRETTY COOL STUFF.
BIG NEWS IS, TODAY'S THE LAST DAY OF THE SAND PAINTING DEMONSTRATION!
THE ARTIST IS A BUDDHIST MONK WHO CAME FROM WAY UP IN THE MOUNTAINS OF TIBET.
COOOOOL!
ALL MONTH HE'S BEEN MAKING A PICTURE OUT OF SAND CALLED A MANDALA. TODAY HE'S GOING TO FINISH IT!
MUSEUM of MODERN ART
AWESOME. BUT, IF SOME PEOPLE DON'T SHUT UP, WE'RE GONNA MISS IT!
SHUT UP!

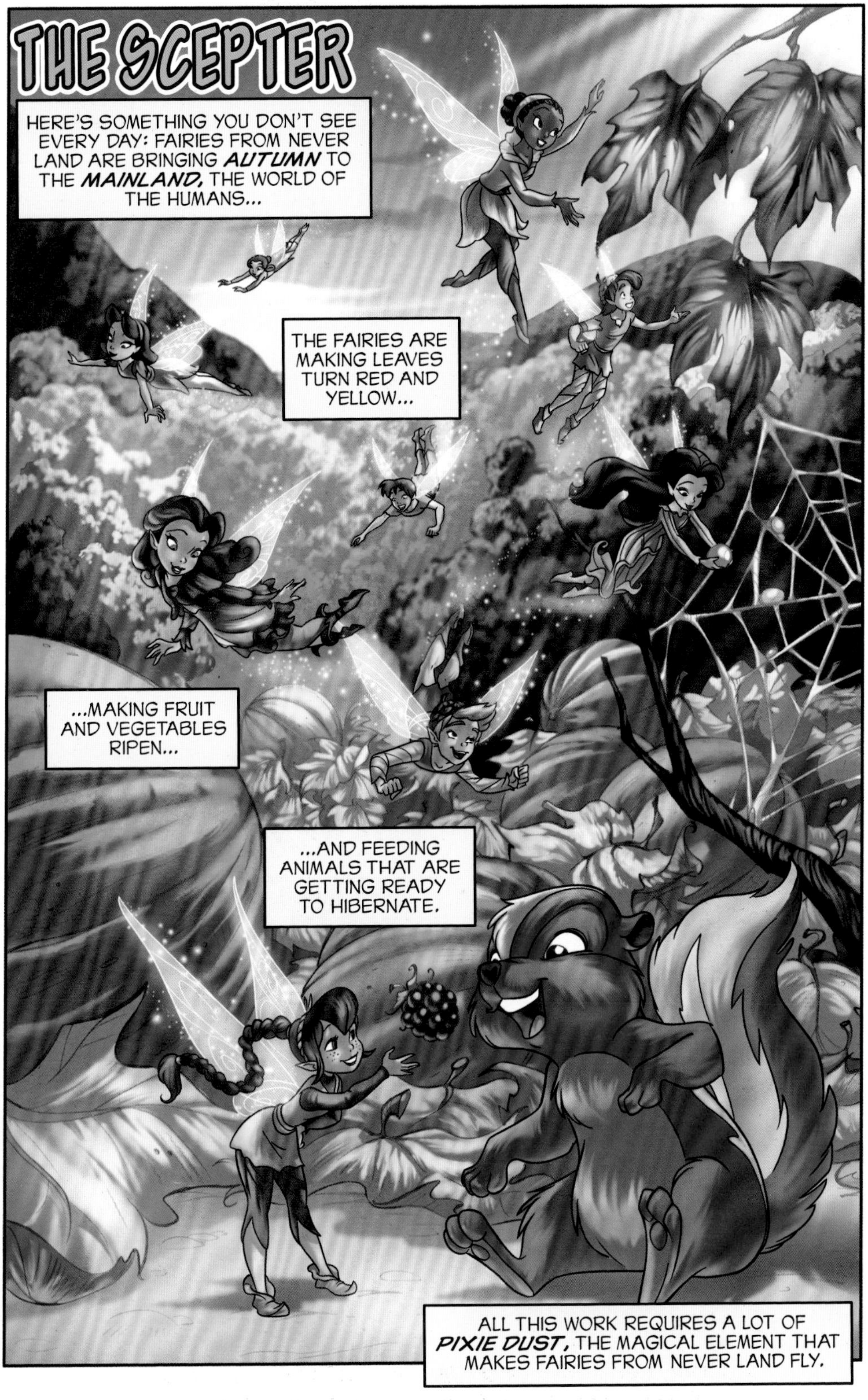
THE SCEPTER
HERE'S SOMETHING YOU DON'T SEE EVERY DAY: FAIRIES FROM NEVER LAND ARE BRINGING *AUTUMN* TO THE *MAINLAND,* THE WORLD OF THE HUMANS...
THE FAIRIES ARE MAKING LEAVES TURN RED AND YELLOW...
...MAKING FRUIT AND VEGETABLES RIPEN...
...AND FEEDING ANIMALS THAT ARE GETTING READY TO HIBERNATE.
ALL THIS WORK REQUIRES A LOT OF *PIXIE DUST,* THE MAGICAL ELEMENT THAT MAKES FAIRIES FROM NEVER LAND FLY.

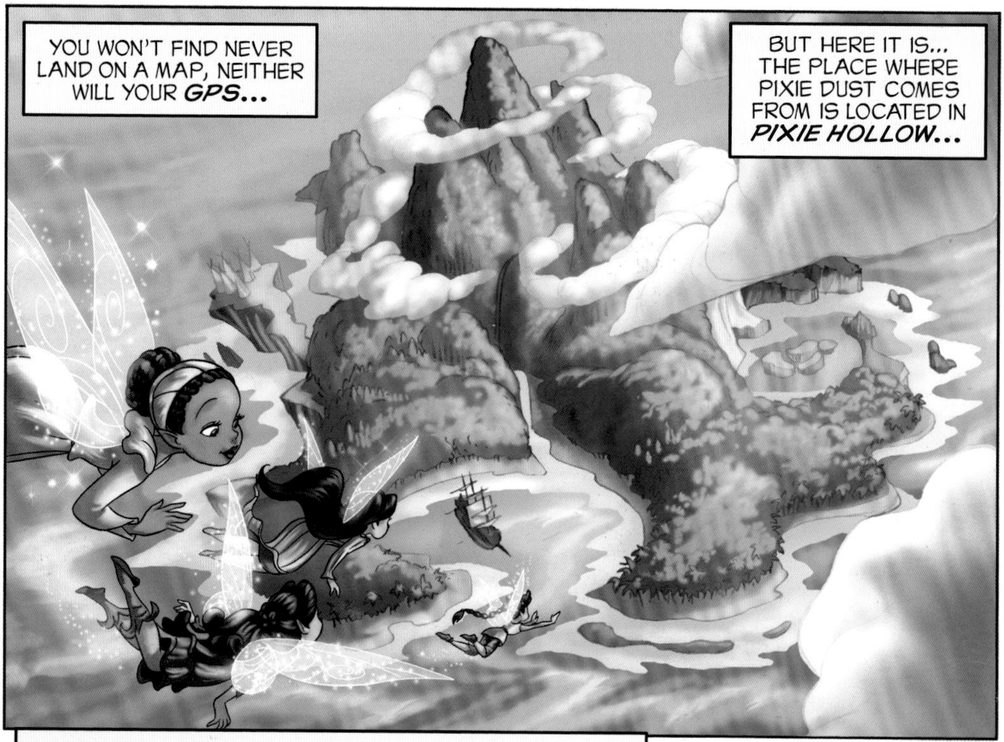
YOU WON'T FIND NEVER LAND ON A MAP, NEITHER WILL YOUR GPS...
BUT HERE IT IS... THE PLACE WHERE PIXIE DUST COMES FROM IS LOCATED IN PIXIE HOLLOW...

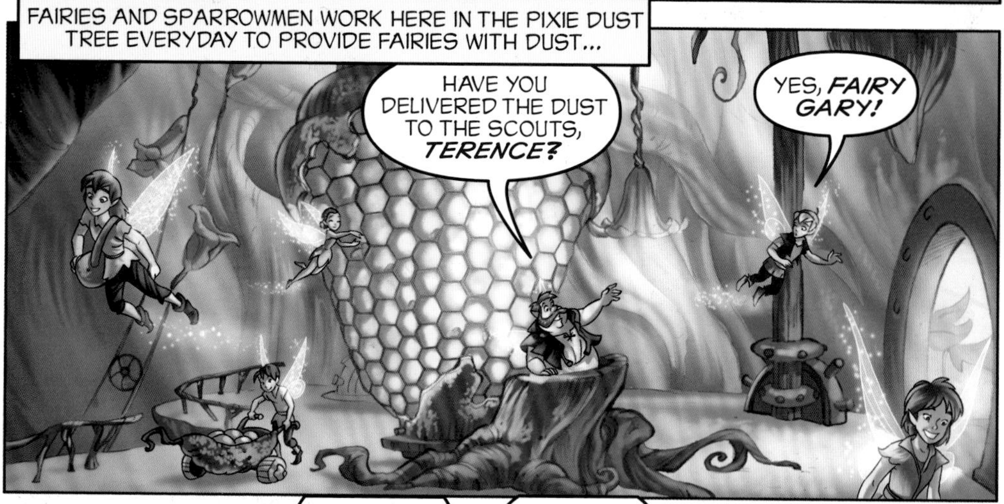
FAIRIES AND SPARROWMEN WORK HERE IN THE PIXIE DUST TREE EVERYDAY TO PROVIDE FAIRIES WITH DUST...
HAVE YOU DELIVERED THE DUST TO THE SCOUTS, TERENCE?
YES, FAIRY GARY!

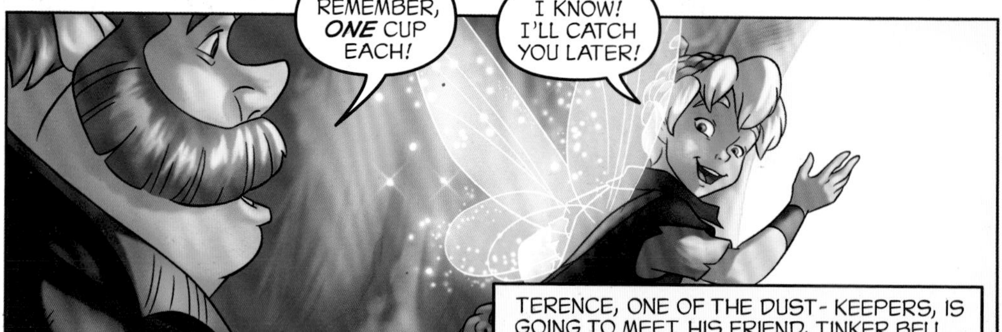
REMEMBER, ONE CUP EACH!
I KNOW! I'LL CATCH YOU LATER!
TERENCE, ONE OF THE DUST- KEEPERS, IS GOING TO MEET HIS FRIEND, TINKER BELL...

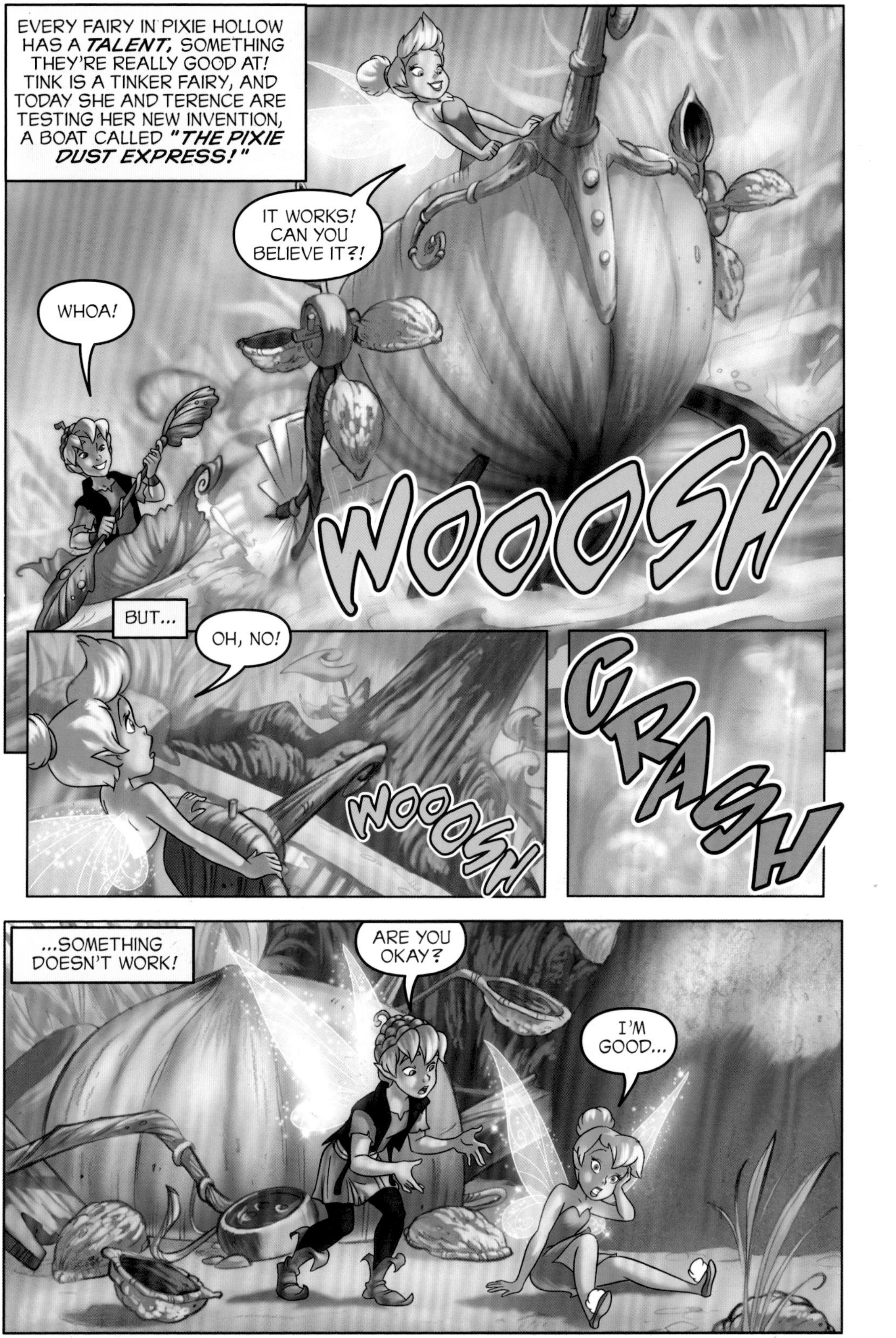
EVERY FAIRY IN PIXIE HOLLOW HAS A TALENT, SOMETHING THEY'RE REALLY GOOD AT! TINK IS A TINKER FAIRY, AND TODAY SHE AND TERENCE ARE TESTING HER NEW INVENTION, A BOAT CALLED "THE PIXIE DUST EXPRESS!"
IT WORKS! CAN YOU BELIEVE IT?!
WHOA!
WOOOSH
BUT...
OH, NO!
WOOOSH
CRASH
...SOMETHING DOESN'T WORK!
ARE YOU OKAY?
I'M GOOD...

Don't miss DISNEY FAIRIES #12 "Tinker Bell and the Lost Treasure"!

More Great Graphic Novels from PAPERCUTZ™

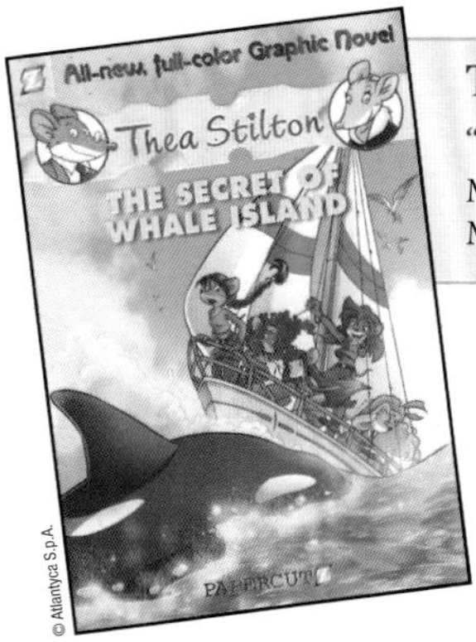
All-new, full-color Graphic Novel
Thea Stilton
THE SECRET OF WHALE ISLAND
PAPERCUTZ

THEA STILTON #1
"The Secret of Whale Island"
Meet the Thea Sisters of Mouseford Academy!

ERNEST & REBECCA #4
"The Land of Walking Stones"
A 6 ½ year old girl and her microbial buddy against the world!

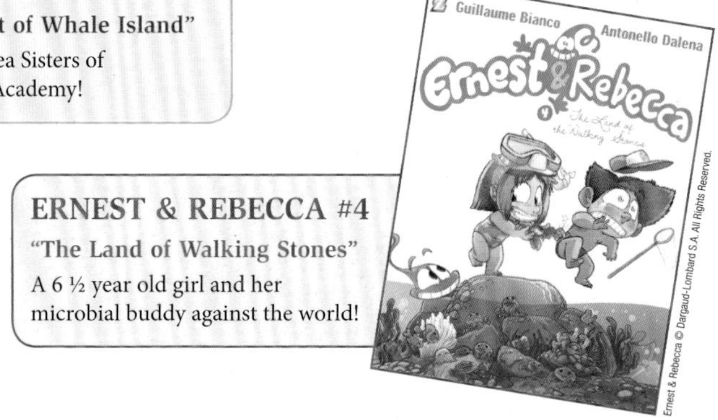
Guillaume Bianco
Antonello Dalena
Ernest & Rebecca
The Land of the Walking Stones

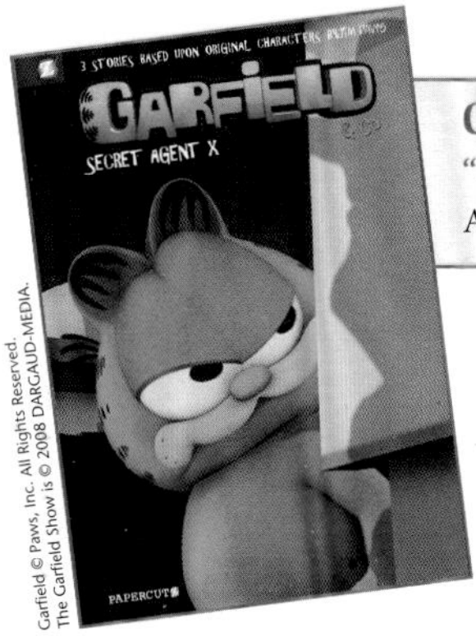
3 STORIES BASED UPON ORIGINAL CHARACTERS
GARFIELD
SECRET AGENT X
PAPERCUTZ

GARFIELD & Co #8
"Secret Agent X"
As seen on the Cartoon Network!

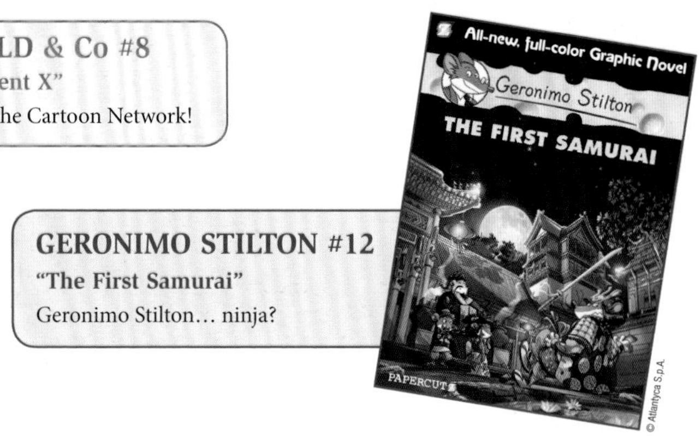
All-new, full-color Graphic Novel
Geronimo Stilton
THE FIRST SAMURAI
PAPERCUTZ

GERONIMO STILTON #12
"The First Samurai"
Geronimo Stilton… ninja?

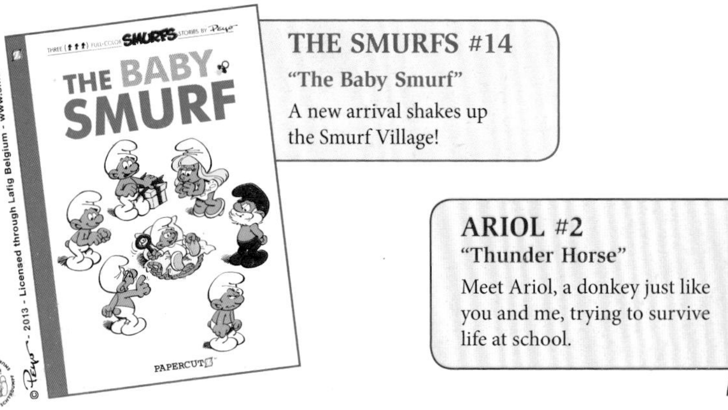
THREE FULL-COLOR SMURFS STORIES BY Peyo
THE BABY SMURF
PAPERCUTZ

THE SMURFS #14
"The Baby Smurf"
A new arrival shakes up the Smurf Village!

ARIOL #2
"Thunder Horse"
Meet Ariol, a donkey just like you and me, trying to survive life at school.

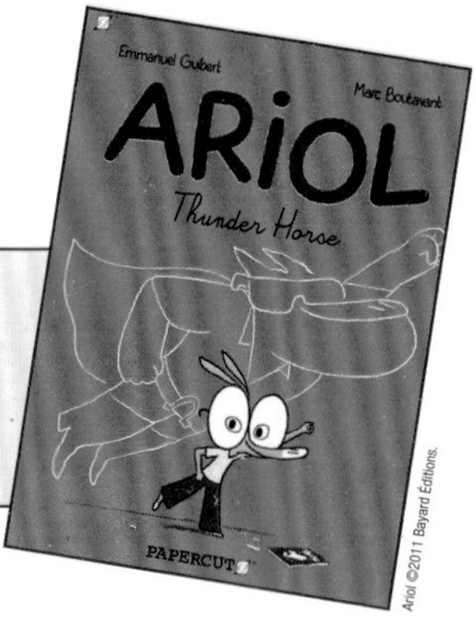
Emmanuel Guibert
Marc Boutavant
ARiOL
Thunder Horse
PAPERCUTZ

Available at better booksellers everywhere!

Or order directly from us! GERONIMO STILTON and THEA STILTON are available in hardcover only for $9.99; ERNEST & REBECCA is $11.99 in hardcover only; GARFIELD & Co is available in hardcover only for $7.99; THE SMURFS are available in paperback for $5.99, in hardcover for $10.99; ARIOL is available in paperback only for $12.99.

Please add $4.00 for postage and handling for the first book, add $1.00 for each additional book.

Please make check payable to NBM Publishing. Send to: PAPERCUTZ, 160 Broadway, Suite 700, East Wing, New York, NY 10038
Or call 800-886-1223, 9AM-6PM EST, M-F